RUNNING INTO FIRE

Magic of Nasci, Book #3

DM Fike

Avalon Labs LLC

For Samantha. Thanks for believing in me back then.

CHAPTER 1

CREATING LIGHTNING OUT of AA batteries isn't as easy as it looks.

Sure, I could suck all the energy out of them like a traveler dying of thirst, but that numbs my arm. Then I'd have to toss the electricity out willy-nilly, like some sort of toddler Zeus. Absolutely no finesse.

That's not what I set out to accomplish. I wanted to hone that power, concentrate it the way I can all the other elements—earth, fire, air, and water. I needed to focus one directed charge at my target, a rotting log, exploding it neatly in the center without damaging anything else in the grassy clearing that overlooked the Pacific Ocean.

I slowly absorbed the AA battery's lightning pith, letting it sizzle up my wrist through to my elbow. I shook my fingers to keep them from falling asleep into that pins-and-needles sensation. With my free hand, I drew zigzags back and forth, a sigil I'd created myself, to focus the lightning pith. I stared at a warped knot in the log, the spot I'd chosen to obliterate from this world.

Beside me, my mentor Guntram scrutinized my every twitch from underneath bushy black eyebrows. He kept his arms folded, bearded chin tucked toward his neck, until the right moment.

"Now, Ina!"

I cried out as I let loose that energy, willing it to form a tight stream of electricity. I imagined it striking the log's knot, exploding the dry tinder into a thousand pieces.

I wanted it to obey me for a change.

Lightning travels too fast for any human to truly observe, not even a shepherd. Guntram and I shielded our eyes as a bright flash lit up the meadow. I heard the distinctive crack of shattering wood. When I opened my eyes to view the damage, I really thought I'd hit my mark this time.

Instead, a twenty-foot-tall Douglas fir towering to the left of the log came crashing down toward us.

Guntram drew a sideways S before my brain cells even registered impending danger. The wind gust tossed me straight into a blackberry bush. It launched Guntram in the opposite direction. The descending tree landed with a sickening thud between us before I took a proper breath.

Ravens squawked in panic above as I struggled to get out of the blackberry's thorny grasp. It clung to my hoodie and shorts, scratching my bare arms and legs as I disentangled myself. Coupled with the berries I'd smooshed, I ended up looking like a disaster survivor, covered in streaks of blood and bright red berry juice.

Guntram popped up from behind the now-smoldering trunk. Glowering, he pointed at my untouched log target. "Again!"

"Seriously?" I pointed at six other burnt-out husks that had suffered friendly fire from my lightning pith practice. "You want me to take the entire grove down?"

Guntram gestured among the sickly trees surrounding us. "A forest fire weakened this area years ago. These firs will not fully mature anyway."

"Still a lousy way to go. Survive a fire just to get blown to bits."

"I thought this is what you wanted," Guntram snapped back. "A chance to prove that you can safely harness lightning."

He had me there. Guntram and I are both shepherds of Nasci, protectors of nature chosen by an honest-to-goddess deity. As cheesy as that sounds, without our magic, monsters called vaetturs from another dimension would overrun our world by sucking up all our natural resources. Our magic comes from absorbing pith from all the natural elements. We draw symbols, called sigils, to redirect that power into a form of our choosing.

Even though I'm an eyas, a shepherd in training, I have the unique ability to wield lightning, a skill no other shepherd has. Some wonder whether lightning should be forbidden because my bolts always manifest as a blunt instrument rather than a surgical tool. Electricity, like me, doesn't take orders well. Guntram and I had been practicing hard the past few weeks to see if we could change that.

"Sure, I'd like to master lightning," I said. "But not at this pace. I'm sure snails could walk the Oregon Trail faster than we're making headway."

Guntram slapped on his lecture face, my least favorite expression. "Anything worth doing is worth taking the time to do right. You have a decent handle on water sigils, but you require more practice with the other elements."

Ugh. Practice. That's all I did lately. If it wasn't lightning sigils, then it was air, earth, or fire ones. Guntram reiterated on a daily basis that I needed to master all the elements for my Shepherd Trial before I became a full-blown shepherd. Not that he would give me a clue as to what to expect in the Shepherd Trial itself or when it might be.

I opened the waterproof pouch that held my extra batteries, the only source of lightning pith I had, and examined their capacity. So far, I'd gone through enough to open my own airport kiosk. I palmed a fistful in my hand.

"We got a problem, Jichan." I referenced the Japanese word for 'Gramps.'

Guntram growled. "Quit calling me that."

Heh. Not a chance. "Even if you wanted to continue torturing me with lightning sigil practice, I'm fresh out of juice."

He sighed. "I suppose we must go back to the homestead."

I did not sigh. We'd been practicing since the butt crack of dawn. Guntram may run on an early bird schedule, but I sympathize with night owls. A break and some food sounded like heaven to me.

I followed Guntram's shredded, hooded cloak as he forged a path downhill. Little puffs of dirt plumed beneath his bare feet as he absorbed earth pith directly from the ground. I chose to wear hiking boots to spare my own feet the endless calluses. To compensate for my own empty earth pith stores, I brushed my legs against bare soil wherever I could.

Regardless of how much I tease Guntram, the truth is, he really does care for me. Given how often I flout orders, most other augurs would have abandoned me as a student a long time ago. But not Guntram. Even though he knew nothing about lightning pith, he had spent countless hours researching what he could, drafting up new ways for me to develop my singular ability. He'd also bent his rigid view of shepherd code to accommodate my ability. For example, he allowed me to visit town to buy more batteries for training purposes.

"I'll need to get more batteries soon," I called to Guntram.

"Batteries," Guntram shook his head in front of me. "Such awful little devices."

And yet, despite his willingness to bend a rule here or there, he had fixed ideas about other things. Like the other shepherds, Guntram pretty much despised human civilization. Not humans themselves exactly, just how they go about their lives. I couldn't blame him for frowning upon how people exploit nature. They destroy Nasci's riches for their own frivolous purposes more often than not, and one-time use items like batteries were especially wasteful.

Too bad I didn't have any alternative. The four regular piths could be obtained by direct contact with nature: air pith through wind, earth through soil, water through just about any body of water, and shepherds could always combine those three elements to create fire pith.

"Hey," I said. "You find a more renewable source of lightning pith, and I'll suck it up faster than a beer gut at the gym. But until lightning storms hover over my head 24-7, I'm stuck with what's available."

Guntram ignored our ongoing argument and swiftly held up a hand, indicating he'd spotted something up ahead. He halted in his tracks, head scanning in all directions. Up above, the kidama ravens that always flew around him also slowed, perching silently in the treetops and cocking their heads to aid in the search.

I came up slowly behind him. "What is it?"

He flexed his fingers at random intervals, caressing the very air itself. "Do you sense that?"

He must have perceived something in the wind, not surprising given his wicked talent with air pith. I raised my own hands to try the same, but all I felt was ridiculous.

"Nope. I'm just standing here violating the air."

Guntram ignored my witty retort, taking a sharp left turn. I followed as he forged a path through some high brush. Wheat-colored barbs poked my already irritated skin. I'd be picking them out of my socks for days.

"This detour better be worth it," I complained.

Guntram stopped again so suddenly, I ran into his back. He grunted in response.

"Sorry," I mumbled.

But Guntram barely paid me any notice. He spread his feet shoulder-width apart in a sigil stance, then crept forward. His actions put me on high alert, and I mimicked his pose. I tried to squeeze past him, but he held me back.

"Let me investigate first, Ina."

I sensed it before I saw it. A buzz in the air. On the one hand, it felt familiar, and yet foreign enough that I couldn't quite place it. It elicited a warped sense of déjà vu, knowledge that I at once knew what was coming, but had also never experienced it before.

We changed directions to track that sensation. It took us across a flat mutilated section of the forest. Someone had obviously camped here illegally. They had chopped down several trees for a dirty fire pit that had burned a bunch of grass around it. They'd left litter all over the place—disposable water bottles, metal lids of food cans, and wrappers scattered about. And in the middle of that trashed site, a shimmering slice of air.

A vaettur breach.

My mouth went dry. Vaetturs create breaches to travel from Letum to our world, usually to hunt Nasci's benevolent animal dryants that keep a natural balance in the world. I'd never witnessed a breach in the middle of such filth, and this one was taller than me by a decent margin and almost as wide.

That made for one large vaettur.

I scanned around to the sides and behind me, looking for the beast, but could see nothing except Pacific coast grasslands interspersed among towering trees that clumped together like middle school cliques.

I asked, "Where's our little friend? I'm ready to go banishing if you are."

Guntram leaned forward, palm inching toward the breach. As his fingers reached within a few feet of the breach, he flinched and stepped backward.

"No," Guntram said. "I'll handle this alone."

I gaped at my mentor. "What do you mean, 'alone?' If it's that big and bad, I should help."

"I don't need your help."

"You're kidding, right?" I detoured around him to place my own palm near the breach. "This vaettur's gotta be huge."

"Ina!" Guntram cried. "Get away from there!"

But it was too late. I'd already opened up my pithways to the flows swirling around the breach.

To say something was wrong would be a gross understatement. A breach normally doesn't feel pleasant, but this one doused my insides with a horrid buzzing sensation. An itching crawled up my spine, coating my torso until it filled up even my airways. I thought I might puke, and my vision blurred.

Guntram slapped my hand away. I gasped as the sensation immediately faded, leaving me weak in its wake. I sunk to my knees.

I stared wide-eyed up at Guntram. "That's no ordinary breach," I said between large breaths, letting soothing air pith push out the awful after-effects from my lungs.

"Which is why I said I'd handle it myself," Guntram growled. "This is beyond your ability. You should go."

As much as that crud inside the breach scared me, I didn't want to leave Guntram alone with this crazy thing. "But what if the vaettur's still running around?"

His furious scowl told me not to ask again. "Go, Ina!"

I gave one last glance at the hazy disc. How ordinary it looked despite its disgusting vibes. Then I turned on my heels and left.

CHAPTER 2

I GRUMBLED OVER Guntram's characteristic lack of explanation as I stomped my way downhill. It sucked being on the lowest rung of the shepherd ladder. Too often I wasn't allowed to know about specific missions or learn sigils of a certain level. This despite the fact I'd fought many powerful vaetturs already, two of which might have killed fellow shepherds without my help. I didn't understand why Guntram blocked me from sealing the whacked-out portal with him.

I soon came across a manmade path, the kind the forest service maintains for hikers. Guntram's nagging voice in my head urged me to walk past it and travel within the relative safety of the woods. Shepherds try to avoid human contact whenever possible. But Guntram had irritated me enough that I opted for the smoother path to my destination.

Besides, who cared if I hiked past one or two people? They probably wouldn't give me a second glance.

I continued to fume as my boots stomped the

comfortable soft bark. The hillside leveled out, and the path widened as two trails merged into one. In my irritation, though, I barely noticed any of this. I didn't even register the crossroads, which is how I ran straight into a backpacker while rounding a stump.

My skull rammed into his chin. He yelped in surprise, and I fell backward in the mulch. As I gathered my wits, I viewed him from the ground up, starting with his muddy sneakers. Toned legs led up to cargo shorts, then a sweat-wicking jacket over a broad chest, hemmed in by modest backpack. But the icing on top of this particular cake was his concerned face. Striking blue eyes peered down from underneath artfully spiked blonde hair. He looked like a movie star on set, waiting for his cue.

"Are you okay?" pretty boy asked, leaning over me.

I gave him a shaky wave. "Besides my ego, yeah," I blurted out. "Sorry about running into you."

"No apology necessary." He extended a hand.

His fingers wrapped around my hand, warm and inviting. He had a strong enough grip that he almost lifted me up by himself, making me feel like I'd used air pith to lighten the load. Breathless, I faced him on my feet, his smile friendly and reassuring.

He gave me a thorough inspection. "You don't have any gear." He dropped his backpack to the ground and unzipped it. "Would you like some water?"

"No thanks."

"But you don't have a water bottle." He removed his own container and took a few big swigs, his Adam's apple rising and falling. The pose showcased his muscled arms, sculpted beautifully in all the right places. He finished by wiping his mouth with the back of one hand.

I gulped in spite of myself, mentally kicking myself for doing so. I couldn't tell pretty boy that I could pull humidity out of the air to drink anytime I wanted.

"I'm fine really," I squeaked. "I'm close to the end of my hike anyway."

He ran a hand through his spiky hair. "This is the middle of the trail. We're miles from the parking lot. How did you get here?"

He was asking too many questions for me to comfortably answer. My mind scrambled for a reasonable explanation. I gestured up the side trail he'd emerged from. "I biked in farther up the trail."

He raised an eyebrow at that. "I didn't think the roads had bike access up there."

Pretty boy knew better than I did. "They don't," I agreed. "My route may have not been terribly, uh, legal."

I thought he would get upset with me. The outdoorsy folk of the Pacific Northwest pride themselves on taking care of their wilderness and disapproved of those who broke the rules. As well they should.

But pretty boy surprised me with a smile. "A rebel. I can relate to that. I'm a bit of one myself."

I wish I could claim I was only "a bit" of a rebel. Most people I know put me squarely in the "insane mutineer" category.

"Yeah, well," I mumbled. "It's not all it's cracked up to be."

He froze me with a frown. "Of course not. They want to keep you down and in your place beneath them."

I snorted, thinking of the other shepherds who often made fun of me because of my unorthodox methods. "Tell me about it."

Pretty boy's lips settled into a conspiratorial smile, which made my heart pound. "Seems like we have a lot in common. Name's Rafe."

"Ina." My shepherd name flew out of my mouth before I could stop myself. I wish I didn't have such a poor filter between my mouth and my brain.

A series of sharp caws cut through our conversation. I stiffened. One of Guntram's birds was looking for me. I needed to leave before I got in trouble for talking to some random stranger. "I probably should get going."

Rafe also cocked his head toward the bird. He paused to stare at me with those unreadable deep eyes. I had no idea what he'd say. I half-expected him to stop me from leaving.

But he finally shrugged. "Have a good hike, Ina." He did not so much as pause as he jogged away.

I slowly walked in the opposite direction, casting glances behind me to make sure he didn't follow. Pretty boy bounced along like he could run around in the forest all day. The solid outdoorsy type with too much stamina to spare.

The raven's caw reminded me I had other issues. I allowed myself one final glance at Rafe, then pushed him out of my mind. It wasn't like I was going to see him again.

CHAPTER 3

I FOUND FECHIN, Guntram's favorite raven, literally hopping mad a short hike away. He jumped from branch to branch, screeching until I dove back into the tree line, away from the trail.

"Yeah, yeah," I muttered up at the stupid bird. "We mustn't ever take the easy route, must we? Gotta make things as difficult as possible." I forged a path toward the nearest wisp channel, the magical portals shepherds use to teleport from place to place. I'd memorized most of the wisp locations in the Talol Wilds so I could zip around the region with ease. That's not to say I didn't miss driving cars, but will o' the wisps were a helluva lot more discrete, especially in remote areas.

Fechin stalked me overhead, not letting me out of his sight. Ever since I'd disobeyed orders to track down a nasty panther vaettur a few weeks back, Guntram had kept his little minion tight on my tail.

I hated having winged babysitters wherever I went.

"You know I'm supposed to pick up batteries,

right?" I called up to the bird. "I'm not heading straight home."

Fechin squawked in reply. Maybe it looked like we were talking, but I had no idea what he said. I can't imprint with Guntram's kidama. Only my augur knew what rattled around their birdbrains.

A series of soft blue pulses flickered ahead at the base of a Sitka spruce. The raven wouldn't be able to follow me through the wisp channel itself, since only shepherds can do that. He would, however, confirm that I'd left the area, and then either he or another raven would fly to the next wisp channel to keep track of me.

But just because Guntram wanted them to watch me didn't mean they could keep up.

I waved at Fechin. "See ya!" I only heard his first shrill note before I leapt into the twinkling lights, the underwater-like silence of teleportation filling my ears.

I didn't pause once my feet hit the other side. Instead, I took off in a sprint, barreling my way through more woods. There were three wisp channels within a mile from here. Guntram's ravens would likely assume that I'd take one that would get me closest to a population center. Instead, I detoured to a channel that would take me to the outskirts of Mapleton, a not-quite-town where I had a secret stash of personal items.

I huffed and puffed as I approached the second channel, glancing at the sky for signs of ravens. I thought I heard one faintly in the distance, but that could have been my imagination. I took the plunge into more pulsating lights before I could confirm either way.

I kept running yet again, away from all wisp channels and toward an old farm property where the ravens probably wouldn't look for me. I sailed out of the forest across an open meadow, the yellow grass crunching beneath my feet. Despite a few early thunderstorms, it had been a relatively mild spring. I took care not to trample any purple camas flowers as I dashed back into the woods.

I maintained a pleasant gait until I reached the dilapidated shed with the turquoise roof that marked the edge of the farm. I strained my ears, but instead of ravens, I heard the sharp bark of a bullmastiff. The dog bared his teeth as he raced from a corner of the farmhouse toward me.

"Hey, boy!" I called. He jumped at me, not to attack, but for affection, front paws planting on my thighs. I bent over to give him a vigorous scruff between the ears. Glancing over at the house, I observed two rusty vehicles and one old pick-up truck in questionable working order. The old hermit who lived here was home. I'm sure he wouldn't have approved of his pooch making friends with a stranger but too bad for him. Shepherds get along with pretty much all animals.

I played with the dog, throwing a stick for him twice before launching it far into the air with pith, where it would take him a while to find. Then I ducked into the shed for the real reason I came.

Most shepherds may shun human civilization and all their comforts, but not me. I love modern amenities. I had a cell phone for a while until Guntram caught me texting instead of doing chores. Fortunately, he didn't know how to turn the phone on, so he didn't know who I'd been communicating with. He'd flip his beard if he found out.

That's why I keep small stashes of hidden goodies all over the Talol Wilds. Sometimes a free spirit wants to connect to the real world. I weaved my way through the shed's cobwebs and battered farm tools to a sagging shelf along the back wall. There, behind ancient paint cans and a massive spider I shooed away, I snatched a satchel filled with single dollar bills. I took out the whole wad and stuffed it in my hoodie's kangaroo pouch. It wasn't a lot, but it would have to do for now. Batteries weren't cheap.

I slipped back outside. I fully expected to run into the dog but not his aging owner, aiming a shotgun at me.

The geezer wore an oversized flannel shirt over jeans held up by suspenders. His once-bright white sneakers were stained with grass. He glared at me underneath his red ball cap. I had to hand it to the geezer, I had not heard him as I rummaged around the shed. Although he was stooped over at an odd angle, he still had a solid steel glint in his eye. He shook only slightly as he clutched his weapon with both gnarled hands.

"Whatcha doin' on my property?"

I held up my hands slowly. I wore a defensive charm which I'd learned from personal experience would stop bullets, but it hurt like a mofo. I preferred not to limp back to the homestead.

"Sorry, sir. I…" I trailed off, not having a good reason to be trespassing. I doubted he would appreciate me using his shed as a hillbilly ATM.

His dog returned triumphant with stick in mouth, interrupting my clumsy reply. Wagging, he trotted right up to me and dropped the twig at my boots.

The geezer's gun faltered. "Rufus!" he snapped. "This here's a stranger. What's wrong with you?"

"Rufus," I repeated with a smile. "That's a great name." I leaned forward to retrieve the stick.

The gun rose back to attention. "What do you think you're doing?"

"Playing fetch," I replied matter-of-factly. "Isn't that what you do with dogs?"

The geezer scowled. "Rufus don't play."

"Is that so?" I pulled my arm back, careful not to make too many sudden movements and scare the old man. "Because Rufus has always played with me before."

"Now see here, Rufus hates everyone. He barely tolerates me. If you believe you can just waltz around my property and do whatever you please, you got another thing coming!"

Ignoring him, I chucked the stick. Hard.

The geezer went slack-jawed as his dog barked gleefully, hunting his wooden prey. The old fart had to turn his whole body to follow its trajectory. I used that distraction to dodge outside his narrow cone of vision, back around the shed and toward the woods.

"Hey!" I heard him yell as I ducked under cover. The distinctive boom of a shotgun blast echoed behind me, but nothing struck my back. The geezer missed me by a mile. Not slowing my pace, I raced through the forest until his cursing faded.

Well, that was more drama than I needed. Much as I loved hanging out with Rufus, I wrote that stash site off for good. At least I'd taken out all my cash. I'd never bother that nasty old dude again.

* * *

I wisped my way to Florence, the seaside town with real retail shops with mostly reasonable prices (for a resort town). Inside a sprawling department store, I grabbed a basket and loaded up on batteries with extra cash left for junk food. The employees gave my mud-caked boots and disheveled hair a few disapproving glances, but they'd experienced enough wilderness bums not to make too much of a fuss. As I walked out the automatic doors, I knew I should return to the homestead.

Instead I sought out one Vincent Garcia.

We had a complicated relationship. Game warden and police officer extraordinaire Vincent and I had met by accident when a vaettur ran amok in his jurisdiction. He couldn't see the vaettur (because non-shepherds can't), so he assumed that

I had poached a bunch of animals. We've since smoothed that all out, and Vincent even helped me track that panther vaettur that attacked us a few weeks ago. Despite this, Guntram forbade me from having any contact with him.

Cough, cough.

So yeah, I'd been texting Vincent when Guntram took my phone. It had been mostly harmless banter. He was someone I could gripe to about shepherd life. He'd filled me in on his life too—the ins and outs of his job that straddles the line between ranger and cop, his strained relationship with his family for taking up a profession they saw as immoral, etc. You know, the stuff friends talk about. Vincent knew where the homestead was (even if he couldn't see it, shrouded in magic invisibility), so I had coaxed him into giving me his address. I'd looked up the location and had it committed to memory, which is how I knew he lived across the street from the department store.

Paper bag tucked underneath my armpit, I dodged coastal highway traffic. My heart pounded, and not because I'd barely missed getting flattened by a service van. I hadn't been able to text Vincent for several days. Had he tried to get ahold of me? Had he even noticed my silence?

Vincent's apartment complex looked new, if no frills, the kind of place bachelors rent. As I bounced up the wooden steps to his second story door, it didn't occur to me until then that he might not be home. I knocked three times. No one answered.

Glancing down at the empty parking lot, most people seemed gone to their 9-to-5 jobs. Vincent worked odd shifts, though. He could be home in ten minutes or ten hours.

Or ten seconds. As I trudged down the steps back to the parking lot, a silver Subaru pulled in. I held my breath as the driver's door opened, and a beige uniform with ebony hair poking underneath a crowned hat stepped out to scrutinize me.

"Ina?" Vincent asked.

I forced myself to play it cool. "Hey, Vince."

He broke out in a bright, relieved smile. "I was worried when you stopped responding to texts."

"Guntram found the phone. He wasn't too pleased."

"Yeah, I bet."

Vincent fiddled with his keys. I shuffled from foot to foot. An awkward silence fell between us.

Vincent finally gestured up toward his apartment. "Would you like to come up?"

"Yes," I replied before he'd finished speaking.

Vincent said something about just getting off shift as he unlocked his apartment, but I barely heard as I eagerly took inventory of his home. It wasn't anything special. The living room had a fold-out futon, entertainment stand with TV and gaming console, and a small, surprisingly neat kitchen with only a few dishes in the sink. He'd placed nothing on the cream-colored walls and piled dirty clothes in a heap just inside the hallway. Vincent left his shoes by the doorway, and I followed his example by removing my boots.

"Sorry about the mess." He used his socked feet to push the laundry back into a bedroom. He then crossed the living room toward a beat-up dining table and held up a paper bag of fast food. "And I didn't bring any for you. I would have gotten French fries if I knew you were coming."

"Maybe we can share." I put down my own offering of chips and pop next to his bag.

Vincent gestured toward the futon. "You want to sit down?"

I glanced down at my clothes. "I'd rather not get your mattress all muddy."

Vincent laughed. "Look who you're talking to." He gestured down to his own similarly stained attire.

"I guess it's a hazard of running around in the woods for a living."

"Normally, I'd've washed right after my shift."

"We should really take a shower," I said. As soon as the words left my mouth, I regretted the unintended double entendre. Whoa, Ina. Phrasing.

Despite the fact that the room remained shrouded in late afternoon darkness, Vincent reddened visibly.

"That came out wrong," I quickly corrected. "Not together. Individually."

This put Vincent at ease. "Oh, okay. You could use the shower first if you want. It's no hot spring." He smiled slyly, referring to the pool shepherds used to heal ourselves. "But there's hot water."

"Really?" I hadn't taken a warm shower since I'd last visited my parents, which felt like forever ago. But I hesitated. "I only have the clothes I'm wearing. It seems kinda pointless to shower if I put on muddy clothes right after." I didn't mention I could shake them down with earth pith if I really wanted to, but that took more effort than I felt like expending.

"If you can stay long enough, you can wash them in my laundry machine. And I'm sure I've got some clothes you could borrow while yours dry."

Now it was my turn to blush. I had not anticipated stripping at Vincent's, even in private. My brain told me I should get back to the homestead before I did something I regretted, while my heart told me to go for it. I bit my lip as they both went to war.

Vincent must have sensed my reluctance. "Not to put you on the spot or anything. I just know how much you miss creature comforts. Consider it an offer from one friend to another."

Using 'friend' did it for me. It had been a long time since I'd had one of those, and I didn't wish to squander it. "Sure," I relented. "Point me toward the shower."

Vincent grabbed a clean towel and spare set of clothes for me, then let me have free reign of his tiny bathroom. There was barely room to close the door, but at least it didn't disgust me. Vincent's pad obviously saw the business end of a sponge on a semi-regular basis, unlike most college dudes' apartments I'd seen. I took a quick shower, basking in the pleasant pressure of millions of water pellets massaging my skin. I would have stayed longer, but I saved some hot water for Vincent.

I cringed, pulling Vincent's fun run T-shirt over my head. It felt intensely intimate and was way too big for me. The sport shorts he'd provided were much less sexy, given they accentuated my chicken legs. Still, I couldn't walk around his apartment naked, so they would have to do.

Afterwards, Vincent helped me start a batch of laundry and showed me how to operate the TV remote before taking his own shower. To my utter joy (and I do not use this term lightly), I surfed through Vincent's cable channels. I missed bad television so much. I grabbed one of my bags of chips and opened a pop, wolfing them down as I watched a serial murder documentary.

Vincent returned in a maroon tank top, a damp towel thrown over his shoulders, while the narrator described the third grizzly murder. He winced as actual crime scene photos of a pixelated body and blood flashed across the screen.

"You like this stuff?"

I swallowed a swig of cola. "You're a cop. This should be your scene."

"You're a nature wizard. You should be watching wildlife documentaries."

"Touché." I pointed to a stack of video games on the entertainment center. "Maybe we should try some of those instead."

He raised an eyebrow. "I warn you, I have no life. All I do is work and play games. You really think you can keep up?"

"If it'll take you down a notch, absolutely."

With the gauntlet properly thrown, we spent the next hour or two shifting through his fighting game collection. Vincent hadn't been kidding about his gamer skills. He beat me handily for the first handful of rounds, but then took pity on me and switched to what he referred to as his B and C string characters. I finally won a few bouts. The banter between us swelled, as if we'd smack-talked each other since childhood.

An unfamiliar contentedness swelled in my chest. Guntram kept my life super busy with shepherd training. I rarely had a moment's rest, much less relaxation. I visited my parents whenever I could, but those were always stress-filled events that left me drained of all emotional energy. Hanging out with Vincent was like taking a break from creating a masterpiece—one-part guilt but four-parts relief.

We lost track of time, only pausing long enough for me to check up on the laundry. We finally gave up when I developed controller calluses on my thumbs, and it hurt too much to continue.

After a quick snack and bathroom break, we ended up sitting next to each other on opposite ends of the futon. "So," Vincent said slowly, not really looking at me, "what really brings you here, Ina?"

I opened my mouth to answer but realized I didn't have an easy reply. It'd seemed natural to let Vincent know I was okay after radio silence, but that sounded too desperate even to my own ears.

I hesitated too long, so Vincent prodded me again. "Come on now, Imogene."

I gave him my best death glare. "Don't you dare use that name."

"Then answer my question."

I decided on a lame fallback. "I was in the area buying batteries."

"Still lightning training with Guntram, huh? Any progress?"

"Not really. I mean, I have no idea what Guntram expects. Lightning isn't exactly known for its controllability. Maybe I will never neatly harness it like the other elements."

"What about the fox dryant? You think he could help?"

"She," I corrected. "And why do you keep harping on that angle? It's not like I can just ring her up whenever I want. Guntram doesn't even believe she exists."

Vincent scooted a little toward me, bridging the distance so that our knees almost touched. "The fox feels like an important element of your history that you're not taking into consideration. Call it police intuition."

I snorted. "'Police intuition.' That isn't a thing."

"Sure it is. We have a sense for certain things."

"Oh really?" I folded my arms. "Like what?"

His eyes softened, making my insides wobble. "Like you weren't just 'in the area.'"

His gaze pierced mine. I couldn't latch onto a complete thought. "Batteries," I breathed.

Vincent leaned forward, his face not far from mine. "You could have picked those up anywhere."

His hand brushed my bare knee, and I swore fire pith pooled in that area. Then his fingers settled on my bare arm, brushing the elbow, and fire did soar throughout my pithways. I couldn't resist him. I tilted toward him as if guided by magnetism, lips softening. A gentle peace overtook me as time slowed to a crawl. Everything felt as it should be.

And as our breaths began to mingle, a shrill ringing sliced between us like a knife.

We jerked away from each other so quickly, I accidentally slammed my back against the wooden futon arm, right in the kidney. Groaning, I rubbed the sore spot as Vincent whipped out his cell phone.

He threw me an apologetic shrug as he answered. "Hello, Officer Garcia speaking."

Apology turned to alarm over whatever the caller told him. He rose to his feet, heading straight for his bedroom without so much as a backward glance in my direction. He closed the door behind him.

I sat there in mild pain and major irritation as I processed everything that had just happened. I'd almost kissed Vincent. A cop outside of shepherd circles. The guy my augur had told me explicitly to stay away from. And then he received a phone call and fled as if chased by vaetturs. What could have caused him to run off so quickly? Did he not want me to hear his end of the conversation? My mouth went dry as I thought it might be another woman, but I tried to push that awful jealousy out of my mind.

"It's a good thing I've already had my period this month," I snarled at the door. "Otherwise, I'd be really upset."

The bedroom door was flung open again, and Vincent stepped out, dressed in a fresh uniform, still talking on the phone. "Got it. Got it. Be right there." Then he hung up.

Ah, now I understood. "Duty calls?"

"Yeah." He scurried over to the kitchen counter containing his wallet and ranger hat. "Wildfire."

That got my attention. I straightened. "Where?" I demanded.

Wildfires were tricky situations for shepherds. While fires are a necessary component to a healthy forest, human mismanagement has made forest fires more dangerous than they should be. According to Guntram, back in the old days, shepherds would let a natural fire burn through a forest with little oversight, since a moderate amount of fire causes certain plant and animal species to thrive in the aftermath. But now, with the forest service suppressing fires in drought-ridden areas for decades, the dry forests are more like sticks of dynamite, waiting to explode. Some animals haven't adapted to these new megafires, and shepherds now must evacuate as many endangered animals as possible from their path or risk losing a precious component of our fragile ecosystem.

"On the edge of Heceta Beach. But don't worry, Miss Shepherd." He threw me a reassuring smile. "A ranger caught it early and stamped it out. No need to call in the nature wizards."

"Oh." I sunk back into the futon, relieved. "Then what's the rush?"

"They ordered me to investigate it since I'm on call. It might be manmade, possibly related to a recent vagrant issue." He wore an expression that I couldn't quite interpret. Regret, maybe? "Sorry I have to run off. It's one of the crappy parts of this job."

"No, I get it." I got my disappointed butt off the futon and checked my clothes in the dryer. They were done. I ducked into the bathroom to get dressed (and use a real toilet one last time) and emerged ready to go.

Vincent herded me out of his apartment and locked it. I jogged down the staircase back to Vincent's car, noting the sun creeping low in the horizon. Wincing, I knew I'd stayed a lot longer than I should have. I didn't relish explaining to Guntram why it took me an entire afternoon to buy some batteries.

Vincent's voice broke through my unease. "I don't mind you dropping by." He leaned over to give me a quick peck on the cheek. "In fact, you should do it again sometime."

I could tell from his smug expression as he drove off that he loved the speechless look on my face. Yet, I'd be lying if I said I didn't enjoy that fiery glow spreading all over my body. Whistling off-tune, I forged a path to the nearest wisp channel.

CHAPTER 4

GUNTRAM DIDN'T EVEN wait for me to return to the homestead before tearing into me. He made an educated guess which wisp channel I'd emerge from and waited for me, boiling over like an unwatched kettle. I materialized out of the blue lights only for his shadow to nearly scare me out of my skin as it latched onto my arm.

"Ah!" I instinctively tapped into my air pith and flung a wind gust in his direction.

Guntram barely twitched his fingers as he countered the air sigil with one of his own. "Where in Nasci's great realm have you been?"

"Yeesh, Guntram," I took a few step backs from his sullen face. "Do you want to give me a heart attack?"

"Only if you wish the same of me." A raven flew down to perch on Guntram's shoulder. "Fechin says you purposely lost him in the woods."

"I told him you gave me permission to take a detour for batteries." I reached into my hoodie pouch to show them to Guntram. "It's not my fault he can't keep up."

The raven shrieked loudly at this, nipping at Guntram's hair. Guntram grunted in response, then said, "Fechin takes offense at having his competency called into question."

"I'm just calling it like it is."

Fechin cawed angrily.

Guntram's face mirrored his bird's. "And if this was only about batteries, why were you gone so long?"

I raised my hands in surrender. "Okay, you caught me. I took a detour for food." I pulled out a smushed bag of chips with a few crumbs left at the bottom. "See?"

Guntram wrinkled his flaring nose. "Disgusting. How you stand consuming that garbage is beyond me."

"What can I say? I'm a shepherd of specific tastes." I hoped I'd covered my tracks well enough that this would end the interrogation. I made a motion to walk away.

But Guntram grabbed me by my shoulder. "You didn't visit him, did you?"

I fought against my quickening pulse. I feigned innocence. "Who?"

"You know who." Guntram's eyes narrowed. "Vincent Garcia."

I decided to answer with a half-truth. "You know I can't get in contact with him. How would I find him?"

"You're stubborn enough to find a way," Guntram answered accurately. "Did you?"

Hell. I had to lie. "No. And even if I did, what's it to you, Jichan? The dude's saved your bacon multiple times now. You know as well as me that without him, you'd either be cockatrice chow or mishipeshu meat." I listed both vaetturs that Vincent had helped me locate, which in turn had enabled me to save my augur.

"He's not one of us. And before you say anything about your parents"—he cut me off with my mouth open—"that's an extreme exception I make given your unusual background. Knowing how much you grumble about them, I'm confident you don't tell them much about Nasci. This Vincent Garcia, however," he lowered his voice, "knows more than he should."

"And has done absolutely zero about it," I pointed out. "Vincent even knows where the homestead is. And yet, have you or anyone else ever seen him around here since?"

Guntram did not answer my question because he knew it would bolster my case. If Vincent really wanted to harm shepherds, he would have done so by now. My augur released my shoulder.

I nodded. "Exactly. So please, don't accuse me of keeping secrets. Not when you openly flaunt yours."

"What are you babbling about?"

"I'm talking about that weirdo breach." Now it was my turn to make Guntram uncomfortable. "What's going on with that, Guntram? What happened with the vaettur that made that thing?"

"I sealed the breach, so everything goes well there," Guntram hedged. "I doubt we'll find the vaettur associated with it, but I have sent word to the Oracle simply as a precaution. It is probably nothing."

The mention of the Oracle made me inhale a sharp breath. She's the lead shepherd of the entire Talol Wilds, the person who calls the shots on all major decisions. Guntram never bothered her unless the situation called for big guns.

"Then it is important!" I cried.

Guntram threw his hands in the air. "Why do you bother asking questions if you never listen? I said, it is likely nothing." Then he stalked away from me.

My augur no longer seemed interested in grilling me on Vincent. Quite the opposite, he wanted to get away from me as soon as possible. It was a victory of sorts, but I couldn't help but jog after him.

"But if it is something, what could that be?"

"You will only hear more if you need to know more," Guntram said with a tone of finality. That's augur-speak for 'shut up, Ina,' so I simply followed his stubborn hide all the way back to the homestead.

* * *

Guntram's avoidance of me lasted all of one evening. He woke me the next day in the pre-dawn hours for a round of sigil practice. We fell into an all-too-familiar pattern—early breakfast at the lodge, then warm-up water practice in one of the homestead's ponds. He kept drilling me on the underwater breathing sigil even though I'd proved beyond a shadow of a doubt that I'd mastered it. Then we rotated through a sigil routine of the other elemental types—a mini-wind funnel, rock fling, and large fireball. The only thing we never practiced on-site was lightning, deemed too likely to cause unintentional property damage.

After lunch, Guntram allowed me a short break so he could spend some quiet time alone in the library. I reveled in this mild reprieve. The home-stead—while crude with its lack of electricity and indoor plumbing—had lots of hidden gems. I could soak in the hot spring to relax. Go back to my room and take a proper nap.

But I ultimately decided to pay Sipho a visit.

Sipho took care of all aspects of the homestead, everything from tending the gardens to mending fences to jarring jam. But she really excelled at for-ging, the art of enchanting objects with pith. She'd crafted the little metal charms that jangled from my neck, allowing me to have extra pith stores out-side of my body, invaluable in a vaettur battle. She constantly tinkered around in her workshop, and in fact, she'd promised me something special when I last left the homestead.

I found Sipho at her forge, a hybrid barn and cabin building near the center of the homestead. Smoke billowing from the brick chimney told me she'd be inside. I'd barely made it across the threshold when Nur, one of Sipho's mountain lions, pushed his light-colored fur up against my legs. Basically a large version of a housecat, I had to pay a heavy scratching toll before Nur would let me pass. Then he plopped back down for a nap on a cushion next to the door.

Sipho didn't notice me at first, her back to the front doors as she crouched over a workbench. She wore a pair of headphones, faint beats of 90s dance music escaping as they crushed her bun braids. Sipho had confiscated my headphones as contraband, but when I demoed their capability, they ended up being her favorite taboo pastime instead. Now I supplied her batteries so she could sway to the rhythm of cheesy tunes when the other shepherds weren't looking.

Rather than calling out to Sipho, which I knew from past experience wouldn't work, I plopped down on a bench across the table. She sensed the vibrations and flinched in surprise, staring guiltily upward.

Until she realized it was just me.

"Ah, Ina." She removed her earpieces. "I saw Guntram slip into the library. I thought you might come by. Behold!" She removed a thumb-sized metallic cylinder from underneath a stationary magnifying glass, one of her crucial etching tools. She had carved tiny sigils I didn't recognize into the cylinder's silvery curves.

Sipho had the proud bluster of a newborn

mother, but I didn't understand the baby. "What is it?"

"This," she paused for dramatic effect, "is a prototype for a lightning charm."

My eyes widened. "What? Shut up! How can you make something like that? I thought I was the only one who could bring on the lightning."

"You forget, a shepherd absorbs pith into their very essence, but a forger like myself merely transfers it."

"Even lightning pith?"

"What is lightning pith to me?" She scoffed. "I can hold it as well as fire, earth, air, or water, which is to say, I can't at all. All I do is enchant objects. I've been experimenting with your batteries." She snagged a wicker basket from the ground, overflowing with AA batteries. "It's taken some trial, error, and not a small amount of research, but I've finally discovered a way to create a charm to hold this unique pith."

I whistled for two reasons. One because I'd had no idea Sipho had so much talent that she could manipulate an energy that even the Oracle couldn't touch, and two because I'm pretty sure all those dead basket batteries represented a month's worth of music juice.

Sipho must have been thinking about the latter because she patted her Walkman. "The only disadvantage is that I'm draining my last set of batteries."

I reached into my hoodie pouch and gave her the

ones I bought in Florence. "This is totally worth the exchange if this thing works like a charm." I grinned at my own joke. "Pun intended."

Sipho ignored my cleverness as she placed the charm into my open palm. "I've managed to fill it with four batteries' worth of pith."

I stroked my thumb across the charm much like I would a battery, zigzagging to charge up its lightning pith. A strong electric current hummed inside. It did indeed feel like quadruple the strength of a single AA.

"That's so cool." I unclasped my charm necklace with the intent of adding this new addition. "I can't wait to try it out."

Sipho frowned and grabbed the necklace right out of my hands. She stood up and strode across the room to a doll-sized set of drawers that held reserve charms.

"Is something wrong?" I asked as she opened up a cabinet.

"Your defensive charm seems a little worn." She removed a thumbnail of metal and added a newer, large one onto my necklace. "It would be better for you to have a completely pristine one. Just in case."

I didn't like the sound of that. "In case of what, Sipho?"

"The lightning charm misfires. The new charm is experimental, so I am sure there will be kinks. We are playing around with Nasci's rarest, arguably most powerful, element. Better safe than sorry."

My enthusiasm for using this so-called lightning charm waned. "Sure, Sipho."

Across the room, Nur jolted awake, his head craned toward the half-open door. He rasped low in his throat before pouncing onto his paws, streaking out the door.

My heart skipped a beat. The cougars guarded the homestead, and they didn't tend to expend unnecessary energy. If something had put Nur on alert, it must be serious. Sipho and I dashed after the cat.

Nur raced toward the plain wooden building that housed the library, Sipho and I not far behind. As if summoned by the frantic feline's approach, Guntram bolted out of the library's doors. He squinted up at the sky, hand held to his temple. A cawing raven appeared above us, diving down toward the ground. The bird spread her wings at the last second to slow her descent and landed smoothly on Guntram's outstretched forearm.

The cougar reached Guntram and curled down to his haunches, waiting as Guntram and the imprinted raven communicated inside their minds with one another. Horror crossed my augur's face. He flung his arm out so the bird could take flight.

"Show me the way!" he commanded. The bird screeched, taking back into the air.

Sipho took a step forward. "What has happened, Guntram?"

Guntram's jaw tightened. "A forest fire. Ina and I must go. Now."

CHAPTER 5

GUNTRAM LED THE way deep into the Siuslaw National Forest that flanked the Oregon Coast's eastern edge. We rushed over pine needles, underneath conifers, and between wisp channels. Another fire. I couldn't help but make a connection to Vincent's sudden emergency call.

"Did a person start the fire?" I asked

"Worse," Guntram called over his shoulder. "A vaettur."

I nearly tripped over a tree root. Sure, there were fire-based vaetturs, but they generally used their fire to capture prey like dryants. I never heard of them burning down a forest. That would kill off a bunch of living things they could snack on. It ran completely contrary to their goals.

"That makes no sense!" I cried.

"Nevertheless, it's true," Guntram said before jumping through a final wisp channel. I leaped after him.

On the other side of the twinkling lights, smoke assaulted my throat and stung my eyes. I drew a fire sigil to lessen the burning sensation, then an air sigil to build a fresh air bubble around my head before I could get a good look at our destination. Despite soot darkening the sky, drizzling bits of ash, I recognized the area as the meadow where Guntram and I had been practicing lightning pith the day before.

"Guntram," I said slowly. "This vaettur-based forest fire wouldn't have anything to do with that weirdo breach, would it?"

"Don't worry about any of that. Other shepherds are dealing with the vaettur."

So basically, Guntram told me yes, this has everything to do with that nasty breach. Before I could ask any follow-up questions, though, the wisp channel light grew bright behind us. We barely had time to skirt out of the way before Darby and Tabitha, the Sassy Squad, materialized.

My least favorite shepherds burst onto the scene like gorgeous lifeguards to the rescue, all choreographed poise and arms up, ready to cast sigils. Tabitha, the taller of the two, removed the hood of her fur-lined cloak, not a honey-colored hair out of place. Her sharp blue eyes assessed every detail of the smoldering forest until they came to rest upon me, the true enemy. She scowled in response.

Darby, for her part, mimicked her augur's scouting routine, complete with scorn in my general direction. Ringlets of platinum hair fell down on each side of her symmetrical face, the spitting image of a high school mean girl.

"What are you doing here?" Darby demanded.

I slapped on an expression of mock confusion. "Gee, I don't know, Darbs. Maybe because there's a fire?"

"Silence," Tabitha hissed at me, before turning to Guntram. "I'm surprised to see you here, given the circumstances."

Guntram puffed his chest out. "I took a vow to protect Nasci as much as any other. I certainly hope you do not believe I would compromise that promise."

Tabitha surprised me by backing down. "No, of course not." But then she threw a thumb over her shoulder at me. "Please tell me she's not here to take on the khalkotauroi."

Guntram shook his head. "We're here for evacuation only."

This appeased Tabitha. "Good. Keep her out of the way. I don't trust her not to make things worse."

I didn't appreciate the implication that I screwed everything up. "Like the time I banished the mishipeshu for you?" I asked sweetly. When Tabitha flashed me a scowl that could wither flowers, I added, "You're welcome."

Guntram palmed his face with one hand, shaking his head, as Tabitha released her full fury. "Jortur would be alive today if you hadn't pulled your little stunt!"

Oh no. I wasn't taking the blame for that one. A vaettur had killed Tabitha's precious deer kidama-turned-dryant, not me. "The mishipeshu could have tracked any of our scents back to the homestead. Don't lay that on me!"

Tabitha nearly knocked me over as she stabbed a finger on my chest. "Then let me lay this on you instead. Stay. out. of. our. way."

And with that, she motioned a smug Darby to follow her. They ran toward the halo of red sky that marked the fire's edge.

I rolled my eyes. "Yeesh. Do you really think they can handle this all by themselves?"

"There's one other shepherd coming to help." Guntram waved me in the opposite direction of where the Sassy Squad had vanished. "Come, we have work to do."

I hated that Tabitha and Darby got to charge into the woods like heroes to stop the khalkotauroi (whatever vaettur that was) while Guntram and I got stuck on evacuation duty. Still, my augur wasn't wrong. Several endangered species called these trees home, and without us, they might not make it out of the forest alive. Biting my tongue, I trailed after Guntram.

Just because we were there to help the animals evacuate doesn't mean they cowered under the onslaught of the oncoming blaze. Animals have good instincts to avoid forest fires, and we found most of them migrating on their own. All manner of birds had already taken to the air to form a bizarre avian highway—from brightly colored swallows to ugly turkey vultures and everything in between. Marine animals like beavers and hoofed creatures such as elk took to streams in species clusters, meandering upstream away from the cause of the commotion. Strings of rodents and other small furry mammals skittered between our feet. The exodus would have been cute except you had to keep your mouth closed for the clouds of flying insects buzzing past. Otherwise, you risked ingesting extra protein on accident.

But not everyone knew when to flee. Like humans, some individual animals have more of a fright than a flight response. We had to coax a pregnant raccoon from a den to get her moving. We drew defensive sigils around a few rare plants, such as Nelson's checker-mallow (I swear I'm not making that name up) that blooms into gorgeous pinky purple flowers in the summer. Guntram did some quick negotiations with a kingsnake stalking a frog, convincing the hungry reptile to forgo a meal in the interest of harmony.

Everything went smoothly until a monstrous owl with a seven-foot wingspan swooped out of nowhere toward us. With wide silver discs for eyes and metallic streaks of mauve at her wing tips, she refused to land, choosing instead to screech above us, an obvious cry for help.

"Sova," Guntram greeted the northern spotted owl dryant. "What seems to be the trouble?"

Sova gave out a trembling cry, then fled inward, back toward the fire.

"Let's go." Guntram spun on his heels, his tattered cloak swirling behind him like a battle-hardened warrior of old.

"Yeah, yeah," I grumbled. That was one big drawback to wearing a hoodie all the time. No superhero chic. I didn't look nearly as cool running after him.

While owls can fly unhindered over terrain, landbound shepherds have no such advantage. We navigated around thorny bushes, fallen logs, and one steep slope to keep up with Sova. Guntram surpassed much of these with a long string of spiraling Ss, sending bursts of air under his feet to launch him up and over obstacles. Not being nearly so skilled with air sigils, I took the more direct approach of "scramble over stuff and suffer lots of cuts and bruises."

That's why I lagged far behind when I heard Guntram give a great war shout. A gale force wind slammed me in the chest, an offensive attack. I had no idea what Guntram fought until I heard a familiar voice cry out against the wind.

"Stop! I'm here to help!"

Vincent? I surged forward with a rush of adrenaline, eager to figure out what the hell was going on.

I leaped into a small grove and nearly had heart failure. Guntram had slid into a sigil stance, a steady stream of hurricane-level gusts streaming from one hand, pinning Vincent against the nearest tree. Vincent, mouth covered in a breathing mask to protect him from the smoke, wore his game warden uniform. He had wrapped both arms around the large trunk for dear life, barely able to maintain a semi-circle grip. He attempted to shout over the wind, but the flow distorted his voice, and he ended up sounding as if talking through a whirling electric fan. Up above, Sova hooted, barely hanging onto a branch in Guntram's fury to blow Vincent straight off the map.

"Guntram!" I screamed. "Knock it off!"

Guntram tossed me a nearly lethal glare. "He's following us!"

How thick was this old man's skull? "No, he isn't! He works for Fish and Wildlife."

But Guntram wouldn't listen. "Sova brought us here. He must be endangering the animals."

"He would never do that!" I cried.

My plea had the opposite reaction I hoped for. Guntram drew another sigil and added a second gale onto the first, blasting Vincent with twice the impact. Vincent screamed above the whistling air as pine needles slapped him from all sides. His feet began to lift off the ground from the wind's force.

Clearly, rational discussion was not getting through to Guntram. Maybe he was worried that Vincent would one day show up at the homestead again. Perhaps he blamed Vincent for a lot of the stubborn decisions I made on an almost daily basis. The reasons didn't matter. I refused to let my augur whiplash Vincent across the forest, possibly killing him, while I stood idly by.

I planted my own feet shoulder-length apart, gathering every ounce of earth in my pithways.

Then, scribbling a square with a slash, I channeled it toward my augur, upending the very ground underneath Guntram's feet.

Guntram had no choice but to relinquish his air attack as the ground flung him to the side. As he fell to the ground, I took the opportunity to race directly in between him and Vincent, who collapsed gasping next to his tree anchor. While a dazed Guntram got his bearings, I rounded on Vincent.

"What are you doing here?" I demanded.

Through a coughing fit, he managed to point up the tree. "Her," he managed.

Vincent seemed to indicate Sova, who had taken back to the air now that the wind had died. She spun in frantic circles.

"You can see Sova?" I asked incredulously. Only shepherds should be able to perceive dryants.

"If you mean the nesting owl protecting her young," Vincent sputtered, "then yes."

That didn't sound like Sova at all. Squinting, I surveyed the tree again and sure enough, more than two-thirds of the way up I could make out a hole in the trunk. A speckled brown head with fathomless black eyes peered down at me, then quickly retreated back into shadow.

Vincent staggered to his feet. "She's got three owlets up there. I haven't seen her partner. He was probably off hunting for the family when the fire broke out."

Sova swooped down toward us, screeching. I

pushed a startled Vincent off to the side so her sharp talons wouldn't scratch him. She barely missed injuring me, only to soar back upwards, hovering around the mother owl's nest.

"That's what Sova's freaking out about," I breathed.

Vincent stared wildly about. "Are there more monsters I can't see again?"

An ominous voice arose behind us. "There are more things that exist than you can dare to imagine."

Guntram had regained his bearings, back on his feet with arms spread out, fingers itching to cast the next sigil. "Step aside, Ina! Or I swear to Nasci, I'll bring you down too."

Before I could reply, a sharp crackle whipped through the forest. Up the hills some distance away, a tree swayed precariously and then crashed to the ground. Its fall sent up a fresh batch of ash raining down on us. I had to redraw the air sigil that allowed me to breathe clean air in the aftermath.

The fire was swiftly heading our way.

"We don't have time for your self-righteousness," I yelled at Guntram. "We need to save the owls."

"Owls?" Guntram blinked. "There's only Sova."

"Guess again." I pointed up toward the tree cavity. Now the mother owl stood outside her nest, her head turned at an extreme angle to gaze at the oncoming fire.

Understanding lit Guntram's face. "She has a nest."

Despite me trying to cover him, Vincent nudged around me to point toward a pet carrier with towels inside that had been blasted into some bushes during Guntram's wind attack. "What do you think I've been trying to do here?"

Guntram's hands fell slightly. "You wish to transport the owlets?"

"Of course." Vincent jerked his chin upwards in exasperation. "They're a protected species. And the mother won't leave without her young."

I took a step toward Guntram. "We need to get them down and into the carrier."

Guntram hesitated. He peered uncertainly at Vincent. "And then what?"

Vincent pointed away from the fire. "I'm getting out of here with the owls. My vehicle's on a forest service road not far away." Then he stared up at the ominous sky. "But you of all people must know how fast fire spreads. We must go now."

Guntram is a lot of things: stubborn, traditional, grumpy. But he isn't a fool. The baby birds couldn't fly yet. The two of us could have carried an owl family around, but it would cost us time to get them to safety, and we had other areas to evacuate. Before I could plead Vincent's case, Guntram drew an air sigil under his feet and launched upward like a rocket.

"Whoa." Vincent backtracked in surprise.

From the ground, we couldn't see exactly what

Guntram was doing, but in only a few seconds, he nestled three downy fluffballs inside the crook of an arm. They peeped as the mother owl perched confidently on his shoulder like a wizard's familiar. Sova stopped screeching as Guntram used his free hand to cast a steady blast of air under his body. He glided lazily back down to the forest floor.

Vincent stared at Guntram as if he'd witnessed my augur spin his head around like one of the owls he carried. "Whoa," he repeated

I poked Vincent in the ribs with my elbow to jar him from his stupor. "Yeah, we get it. Guntram's a show-off."

"But how do the owls trust you enough to let you do that?"

Guntram bristled. "All animals trust shepherds. It is you they do not trust."

"But they should." I waved at Sova, who had flown down to our level. "Vincent's okay, I promise. He'll get the family out of here safe and sound in his little box." I pointed to the carrier.

Sova hovered nervously, not sure how to proceed. This caused the mother owl to cry out in objection. I knew if the dryant didn't agree to go with Vincent, we'd be forced to carry them ourselves.

But Guntram surprised us by turning to Sova and saying, "On my word, this man will aid you. Allow him to place the owlets in his crate."

This placated Sova, and thus the mother. They allowed Guntram to gently lay the owlets inside the towel folds. The mother then insisted on staying with her children, which Vincent allowed, locking the cage behind her.

Standing up, Vincent and Guntram faced each other. Guntram slapped a hand on his shoulder. Hard. "Promise me you will release them soon."

Vincent nodded. "I'll get them out of the fire's range. It'll be a short ride."

Guntram still appeared skeptical but said to Sova. "I've given you my word, but you must follow them to soothe the mother."

Sova screeched in affirmation.

With the air quality rapidly declining, Vincent didn't linger. He only spared me a quick, "Be careful."

I gave him a tight nod in return.

Then he fled down the hillside, Sova an invisible ghost tailing him to ensure he didn't break his promise.

CHAPTER 6

THE INFERNO SURROUNDING us worsened. After Vincent disappeared from view, the heat from the encroaching fire rose several degrees. I absorbed fire pith to take the edge off it, releasing it just enough to keep me cooler but not enough to overwhelm my other internal pith stores.

Guntram must have done the same thing because a flicker of flame sizzled in his irises as he said, "We've got work to do."

We cut a path perpendicular to Vincent's escape route, back toward where we'd been before Sova found us. Out of nowhere, the fire lurched in a new direction. Fires can travel crazy fast, sometimes faster than a person can run, and more horrifying than that, they can "jump." One moment, we were well ahead of the flames, traveling at a decent clip down slope, and the next, a tree in front of us caught fire like a matchstick. Some chunk of lit debris—probably a twig or branch—had caught a breeze and floated above our heads, landing on its crown. The tree sparked, causing a secondary blaze that set the dry grass around it ablaze. Streaks of flame formed a line in front of us, blocking our path.

Shepherds can absorb fire pith, so this wasn't a death sentence, but it wasn't a walk in the park, either. Walking through open flame is tricky but doable for short stretches. Guntram could handle an extended immersion, but I couldn't. I'd never stood in a fire for more than five minutes, and that forced me to relinquish all other elements in my pithways to create a continuous cycle of absorbing and releasing fire pith. It exhausts the body quickly, and if I couldn't keep it up, I would end up crispy like anyone else.

"This way!" Guntram cried, attempting to re-route us around the new blaze. We broke out into a run, hoping to circumnavigate the new fire before the old one caught up.

We might have even made it, too, if the khalko-tauroi hadn't shown up.

A roar sounded behind us, louder than even the tidal-like crashes of the fire. A thick wall of purple haze accompanied it, making it hard to see even my own hands stretched out in front of me. As it overwhelmed my air pocket, I sputtered, gathering what little air pith I had left as oxygen to breathe. I could hear the sounds of scuffling and trees falling around me but was completely blind in the smoke.

"Guntram!" I called, trying to orient myself.

Over the din, a raven squawked. I shifted in that direction, stumbling until I came back out into relatively clear air.

That's when I came face-to-face with the bull vaettur.

It stood in front of the forest inferno, ground to sky bathed in a sharp, flickering orange light. Skeletons of trees twisted unnaturally behind it, horrified victims of the fire's demise. The copper-colored bull, almost twice as tall as me, roared again, its eyes a hot blue-white. Smoke trailed from its nostrils and mouth, the source of the forest fires. The raven's caws I thought I heard were actually the sound of branches snapping off trunks around the bull like bits of confetti.

I yelped and jumped backward, expecting the bull to charge.

Seconds passed. Nothing. The bull pawed the ground. Although his gaze had me pinned, he seemed to look straight through me.

I'd fought a lot of vaetturs as part of my training, and not a single one of them swayed in in a trance-like state. I raised my hands to attack the bull with water, but that seemed cruel somehow, like stabbing a sleeping crocodile.

Darby, however, had no such qualms. She flew sideways in front of me like an avenging angel, her hair for once tangled in the wind as she launched a whirlwind around the bull, creating a mini-vacuum where it stood.

This caught the bull's attention. It staggered toward Darby, now situated directly in front of me. Its mouth opened for a cry that broke the whirlwind. Fire burst from its mouth, aimed squarely at us.

I raised both palms to absorb the fire but had already reached my pith absorption limit. Fortunately, Darby had no problem intercepting the entire bus-length stream of fire. She redirected it back at the bull's hooves like an unwieldy whip.

I stood in stunned amazement, watching her fingers fly through an array of fire sigils. I didn't have the chops to pull off that ballsy of a move. A distinct white-hot aura radiated all around her as she fought, indicating she could stand inside the flames for quite a while. Now I knew why she'd been allowed to track the vaettur, and I'd been stuck on evacuation duty.

A hard smack between the shoulder blades jolted me back to my senses. I whipped around to find Tabitha, also covered in a glowing aura. Globs of steaming water followed her around, distorting her face as I peered at her between their floating surfaces.

"Haggard!" Tabitha screamed at me. "Get out of here!"

Tabitha shoved me. As I stumbled, I opened my mouth to yell at her, but then another cloaked figure emerged out of the flames, a calm phantom. Wearing olive green from hooded cloak to flowing pants, the smoldering red bracelet on her slender wrist popped out as the one bright bit of color. I couldn't see her face until she was nearly upon me, and even then, her deep complexion made it difficult to discern anything save those intelligent eyes. They observed every detail, calculating her moves as if part of a massive game of chess.

Azar. I'd only met her a handful of times, but it had been enough for me to respect her. She had a mind like a sponge, never forgetting anything she saw, heard, or read. She learned most sigils, even complex ones, on her second or third try. But perhaps her most astounding ability was her fire sigil execution. As the combination of water, earth, and air combined, fire pith had the earned reputation of being the most difficult basic element to master. I'd watched Azar practice with a bonfire on the homestead. She could pull off moves even Guntram couldn't do, like creating a bird out of flame that she could control as her own personal drone. She hadn't become an augur yet, but despite her relative youth, it was only a matter of time.

Azar paused only for a moment to say, "Give us space, Ina."

I obeyed in a daze, scurrying out of the way as Azar marched right up to the defiant Darby facing the snarling copper bull. Darby may have been bold, but she was on the verge on losing the bout of fire volleyball. A side stream of fire bounced off her aura and struck her on the ear. Darby cried out in pain, her fingers faltering.

Tabitha's hands, swirling with water sigils, couldn't help her eyas without letting her floating water orbs evaporate. "Azar!" the augur snapped. "Get on with it!"

But Azar didn't need Tabitha's permission. She'd

already slid her legs apart, arms circling in front of her as she worked her fingers through several rapid-fire sigils. I didn't understand her strategy until the bull began to choke. Its fire stream on Darby lessened, diverted instead to Azar's graceful movements. The bull's sputtering soon turned to outright panic as fire shot out of its mouth involuntarily like a leaky faucet, obviously no longer under the vaettur's control as it formed streamers of fire around the almost dancing Azar. Darby, relieved from the assault, fell exhausted to her knees.

When the last bit of flame sputtered from the bull's lips, Azar shouted, "Now!"

Tabitha sent her water globs straight toward the bull, as sharp and fatal as any arrow. They pierced its thick hide, sending the khalkotauroi into howls of agony.

Then Tabitha brought out the pièce de résistance, a five-pointed star. The water orbs sunk farther into the bull as Tabitha let loose her banishment sigil. The smoke intensified around the vaettur, not because of the fire, but because it was melting. Bit by bit, it lost fur, limbs, and finally its snouted face until it vanished in a cloud of putrid smoke.

CHAPTER 7

NORMALLY OUR JOB is finished when we banish a vaettur, but given the khalkotauroi had activated a forest fire, we had to stamp it out. Guntram caught up to us, and with two augurs and an accomplished fire shepherd, it only took a few hours to get everything contained. Guntram deprived oxygen from large patches of ground using air sigils, choking the larger flames to death. Azar and Tabitha accomplished the same thing with fire suppression, redirecting the fire's path to places where it had no more fuel. Darby and I offered water service by soaking up water pith in nearby streams and bringing it back to dampen the flames.

About the only hiccup we experienced was hiding from the occasional government helicopter splashing down chemicals to stop the blaze. This ruffled Tabitha since it sometimes interfered with her fire redirection, but what could you do? At least normal people cared enough to try. All five of us also purposefully avoided the western front of the blaze, where a group of on-ground firefighting trucks held the line. We made sure we weakened the fire so much they'd have to be idiots not to finish extinguishing the last 10% themselves.

By the time we returned to the homestead, my lungs felt like someone had painted them over in a thick layer of sludge. All I wanted to do was soak in the hot spring, a very reasonable request, so I slinked off in that direction.

"Haggard!" Tabitha's shrill words beckoned me. "Debrief at the lodge. Now."

I flipped around, gesturing toward my ash-laden clothes. "Can't it wait until we've recharged?"

"No," she snapped. "Not unless you intend to put more dryants in danger."

I cocked my head at her in confusion. "We put out the fire. What's the rush?"

Tabitha looked like she wanted to slap me, but Guntram intervened. "Just do as directed, Ina."

I might have continued arguing, but Azar stood next to us, calmly watching the exchange. I didn't want to come off like a jerk in front of her, so I bit my tongue and trailed everyone else into the lodge.

What the lodge lacked in modern amenities, it did make up for in a cool layout. Because shepherds thrived when constantly absorbing the four elements of Nasci, the common area had a dirt floor, a constant-burning fireplace, small glassless windows for natural air flow, and a wading pool built into the ground. We sat on the outer stones of the pool, letting our bare feet soak in the lukewarm water. I wriggled my toes, absorbing water pith to wash out the annoying excess of fire pith still stored in my system. Not as good as the hot spring but an okay second.

Tabitha reminded me quickly I wasn't there to relax. "Before we begin, let me remind you all that certain members present do not have authorization to discuss crucial details." She glanced pointedly at me.

I curled my hands into fists. Tabitha loved to pull rank. "Then why even bother having the eyases here?"

Guntram answered. "Because it's worthwhile for everyone involved to review a vaettur encounter so those in charge can make informed decisions."

What a jab at my intelligence. "C'mon, Guntram. It doesn't take a brain surgeon to figure out that this is related to that weirdo breach we found yesterday."

While Guntram and Tabitha glared at me, Darby cocked her head to the side, puzzled. She obviously hadn't heard anything about what Guntram and I had found yesterday.

I decided to forge ahead for her benefit. "That breach radiated the heebie-jeebies and you know it."

Tabitha cut me off. "That is not up for review." She faced the others, disregarding me like a child. "We only need to discuss the khalkotauroi. Starting with Darby."

Darby stiffened so rigidly, I worried her back would snap as she gave her recollection of events. She described chasing after the bull, how it didn't exhibit any patterns in its behavior, charging about aimlessly, sometimes starting new blazes, sometimes not. Azar and Tabitha followed up with similar stories. Together, the three had tried multiple strategies to hem in the vaettur for a final one-two punch of fire suppression and water banishment. But the khalkotauroi's movements were so erratic, they couldn't predict where it might go next, sometimes attacking them, sometimes avoiding them, but never letting anyone get close enough to stop it.

While Tabitha, Guntram, and Azar accepted these behaviors as facts, I had a hard time wrapping my mind around it. Vaetturs lived to hunt. The khalkotauroi should have been stalking animals or dryants. Starting fires ran counterintuitive to that objective, causing most living creatures to flee in the opposite direction.

I asked, "You're saying our bull went on a completely directionless arson spree?"

Azar folded her hands neatly in her lap. "So it would seem."

I pressed on. "And what about when I found it? The thing just sat there staring off into nothing, almost catatonic. What's up with that?"

Although Darby nodded in agreement, the three older shepherds didn't appear worried about the vaettur's odd behavior. Guntram confirmed as much when he whispered, "Let it go, Ina."

I slouched backward, angry, not caring if the others noticed. It was clear I wouldn't get any answers from the so-called wise elders of this group. Instead, I pursed my lips as Guntram retold his perspective of events, listing all the species we'd helped during our evacuation.

I'd almost closed my ears to the entire charade when Tabitha asked Guntram, "So, you did not run into anyone in the forest during evacuation?"

My heart dropped as Guntram replied, "We did."

In the chaos of fighting the bull, I'd completely forgotten about Vincent. Knowing how much Guntram hated Vincent for his role in my recent misadventures, I expected him to rake the game warden over the coals. I had no idea how much the other shepherds knew about Vincent and my relationship, but I really did not want it coming to light here, in front of a self-righteous Tabitha.

Guntram continued. "We ran into a forest service ranger attempting to save a nest of northern spotted owls. We made sure he carried the family out of the fire's range, with Sova monitoring him for us."

I had to hold my jaw tight to keep it from dropping open. That was the most benign way of putting our encounter with Vincent. Not only had we had a full conversation with Vincent, Guntram had attacked him. Yet, my augur revealed none of this.

Tabitha noticed my fidgeting and addressed me.

"Is that how you remember it?"

I nodded curtly, not trusting my voice.

Her gaze ripped through me a few more seconds before she focused back on Guntram. "And you swear that you did not know this man?"

Guntram appeared offended at the question, his beard bristling. "I'd never seen him before today," he said truthfully. Only his raven kidama had met Vincent.

"And you ran into no one else that you knew?"

"Of course not." Guntram's voice rose in a way that I rarely saw in front of anyone but me. "Do you think I would withhold such information given what's happening on Mt. Hood?"

Azar piped in. "No," she said gently. Her eyes pierced Tabitha's. "No, we do not."

Tabitha didn't exactly seem contrite at this double defense, but she did back away. "It's a question worth asking."

Azar seemed eager to defuse tension. She turned to me and asked, "Do you have anything else to add, Ina?"

"Besides the fact that none of this makes a lick of sense?" I countered. "Nope. I'm good."

"Then I adjourn the general debrief," Tabitha declared. "Let us move onto strategy planning. Those of a lower rank," she gestured toward me, "should leave."

"Perfect." I jumped to my feet. "I'm happy to ditch all this redacted red tape anyway."

I stole a quick glance at Guntram, who was too

lost in his own thoughts to chastise me. I was too angry to wonder what that could have meant. I nudged past Darby, who stood ramrod at attention for a flurry of orders from Tabitha, and stalked out of the lodge.

CHAPTER 8

I SHOULD HAVE gone for a soak in the hot spring. Heaven knows I felt cranky enough that I needed to soak away my bitterness. But when I'm mad, I don't always make the most rational choices. Instead of recharging for whatever lay ahead, I decided to stick it to all the mightier-than-thou shepherds back at the lodge and take a walk off the homestead.

Technically, it's not against the rules to wander off by myself, although Guntram heavily frowns upon it. I figured I'd be ok picking up more batteries since Sipho had depleted my supply. So I located all of Guntram's resting ravens (except Fechin, who seemed mysteriously absent), snuck past them, and jumped into the nearest wisp channel.

This brought me close to Carol and Dennis's highway rest stop, a rundown convenience store and fueling station for the handful of rednecks that lived this far in the Cascades. I came here often under the guise of being a lecture-ditching college student. Occasionally, a hapless tourist stops by to do something adventurous like use the restroom, and I get some bonus entertainment with my purchase.

Today was one of those lucky days. I smirked at the electric hybrid sedan in the dirt parking lot, looking as out of place as a diamond ring inside an arcade claw machine.

I stepped into the shop. Dennis stood behind the cash register, arms folded on top of overalls and a sagging beer belly. Opposite him slouched a 30-something hipster with a flannel shirt, mirrored sunglasses, and a leather phone holster. A fluorescent light flickered over a bag of processed goodies between them.

The hipster rubbed one manicured finger on his temple. "How can you not know what kombucha is?"

Dennis answered in a low voice that would rather be smoking a cheap cigarette. "I ain't that kind of business," he said with a hint of disgust.

The hipster snorted in superiority. "Do you even carry anything locally sourced?"

"If by locally sourced, you mean Chuck Johnson down the road restocking the coolers a couple times a month, then the whole place is your oyster, kid."

The hipster sighed in superiority. "Clearly, we're not even on the same level here." He stepped toward the exit but found me lingering in the doorway. He must have mistaken my casual attire as a sign of a kindred spirit because he said to me, "I'd turn around if I were you. I doubt this servant to corporate America even knows what organic means."

I slapped on a bright smile. "You mean like potato chips? They grow in the ground, right?"

The hipster finally noticed the mud and soot stains on my body. He sniffed, wrinkling his nose as if catching a whiff of something funky.

I decided not to let this chance go to waste. "I took Chem 101. Anything with carbon atoms counts as organic, right?"

His camaraderie faded to mumbles of derision as he slid past me out the door.

Dennis's scratchy chuckles added a strange harmonic vibe to the rusty chimes on the glass door. "Good one, Ina."

The owners knew me as the college kid from Eugene who played a lot of hooky in order to hike around the mountains. They found me strange but tolerable, especially since I took a more practical approach to life than a lot of crunchy people from 'the big city.'

I gave Dennis a half bow on my way to the dustiest shelf in the far back, where all the non-perishables were stored. "Glad to be of service."

I'd made it halfway past the ancient cans of soup when Dennis said, "If you're looking for batteries, I'm sorry to disappoint you."

I flipped around, only the top of Dennis's thinning white hair visible behind the metal shelves. "Are you out?"

"Haven't bought more since the last time you

came in."

I dragged myself back to the counter, stifling a groan. Now I'd have to go out of my way to buy more. "Dennis, you're killing me here."

Dennis shrugged. "You're the one who keeps buying us out of stock. The suppliers can't keep up. What're you using 'em for, anyway?"

I said the first thing that came to mind, not knowing if they used AA batteries or not. "Vaping."

Dennis made a face. "I heard that stuff will kill you."

I squelched the urge to give him a lecture on his own long-term nicotine use. "Well, I guess I'm off to the next place then. If you want to stay in business, you need to cater to your loyal customers."

Dennis dismissed me with a wave. "If I listened to all you youngsters, this place would be filled with kumbuttya already. And I may be set in my ways, but I ain't never sold porn here, and I never will."

* * *

I considered returning to the homestead. I had the lightning charm, so it wasn't like I had absolutely no lightning pith. But one-upping a hipster hadn't blown off enough steam, so I opted to take a trip into the very place Dennis scorned.

The greater Eugene area is quite a bit larger than the little rural towns surrounding it. Much smaller than the state's larger Portland metro area, Eugene still boasts a major public university, two malls, and tons of box retailers, making it an ideal place to buy cheap batteries. I opted to take the fewest wisp channels into town and ended up not far from local landmark Spencer's Butte, an isolated knoll with a rocky top with a popular hiking trail snaking off it. I headed north on the longer path leading back into town, aiming for a grocery store inside a strip mall nestled within the city's southern hills.

I meant to grab batteries and a fresh snack to go that, unlike at Dennis's, hadn't been sitting on a shelf since before I was born, but that all changed when I noticed a Scottish-themed brew pub next door to the supermarket. A sign boasted a happy hour in full swing and some cheap eats. I bought my batteries quickly and decided to surrender my appetite to the whim of the bar.

Despite its distance from the university, the pub crawled with a decent sized college crowd. I discovered why when I noticed a digital clock stating it was Friday evening. The dawn of party time. Bantering co-eds in sports apparel had taken up all the pool tables. A mob three-people thick lined the counter as the bartenders rushed to fill orders. Most of the tables already had people huddled around them or a backpack to mark their territory. All around us, large LED TVs flashed snippets of various basketball game highlights.

I didn't have an ID for alcohol, but given the average patron age, hoped I could order a hamburger without question. I wedged myself up to the bar and waited impatiently as hordes of rude millennials cut in front of me anyway.

I was beginning to wonder if I should go back to the homestead when I spotted familiar ebony hair over a maroon athletic T-shirt. Vincent Garcia, who should have been miles away in Florence, stood from a table near the door with a smiling brunette in a trendy leather jacket. Her bright eyes sparkled with something she had told Vincent. He leaned forward to speak closer to her soft face. Maybe they couldn't hear each other over the noise of the pub, but they seemed cozy too. He kept his hand at the small of her back as he led her outside into the parking lot.

A flood of emotions raked throughout my body. What was Vincent doing here in Eugene? Who was the chick? I replayed the scene in Vincent's apartment only the day before. Had I been a complete and utter idiot letting Vincent get that close to me?

I pushed a few protesting pool players out of the way in my haste to follow, but even so, the sheer number of people made it difficult to navigate. By the time I got outside, Vincent's silver Subaru had turned onto the street, too far away for me to catch. But I caught a glimpse of the brunette leaning over and pecking Vincent on the cheek. The last I saw of them, her fingers lingered on his face.

I'm not sure how long I stood there, gaping after them. I clenched and unclenched my right hand to prevent fire pith from exploding onto the sidewalk. I wanted to lob a steady stream straight at Vincent's head.

A tattered homeless man lounging in front of a nearby liquor store yelled me out of my stupor. "Missy! You spare me some change?"

"Oh, things are going to change," I muttered under my breath. Then I stalked off, back toward the wilderness.

CHAPTER 9

I RETURNED AT dusk to the homestead. The meeting at the lodge had already broken up. I expected Guntram to pounce on me the minute I showed myself, furious that I'd left the grounds without notice. When he didn't manifest in a tirade, curiosity got the better of me. I noticed a glow coming from the slightly ajar library door. Peeking inside, I could just make out Guntram's cloak hunched over a stack of books at one of the desks.

As I slowly backed away, I thanked my lucky stars that Guntram was distracted. Hot flame still threatened to explode out of me when I thought of Vincent, and I really needed to decompress. I took my alternating depressed and enraged self down to the hot spring to soak away my misery.

While the waters did wonders for my physical weariness, it did little for my overall mood. I couldn't shake the vicious cycle of thoughts that ran like a hamster in a wheel through my brain. It started with betrayal. How could Vincent lead me on, up to almost kissing me in his apartment? But then I reminded myself that I was the one who'd showed up unannounced at his door. He hadn't been pursuing me. Sure, he'd texted me for weeks, but he never strayed into concrete romantic territory. I'd made sure of that. That's when I berated myself for acting like such an idiot around some guy. Then my mind focused on the brunette. She obviously knew Vincent well. Were they dating? How could I, a secretive forest rat, compare to someone Vincent could call up at a moment's notice? A familiar stirring of longing surged in my chest, only to be replaced by the scene on Vincent's futon.

And so the cycle continued.

By the time I trudged out of the pool, night had completely fallen, bringing a chill breeze that forced me to expend pith to stay warm. The last thing I wanted was to deal with other people, which is why of course my path had to cross Tabitha and Darby. They had created an enormous bonfire in one of the homestead's many fire pits. Darby stood in the center of it, surrounded by a fading white-hot aura. She kept her eyes closed, lips trembling as her fingers drew shaking crosses to keep the blaze from consuming her.

"Steady!" Tabitha barked from the sidelines. "Don't let up, not even for a second!"

Poor Darby. She'd held her own against the khalkotauroi, and yet here she was, overworked under the strict hold of the worst tiger mom in all the Talol Wilds. The way Darby's motions came out, stiff and erratic, she wouldn't hold up for much longer.

"Can't…" she wheezed, and by doing so, paused long enough in drawing sigils that her tunic caught on fire. She yelped, fingers jerking to douse it. I could see bits of smoke coming off her skin, a sign that she barely had the blaze in check.

"You will!" Tabitha yelled back. "Or you will die!"

I couldn't stand there and watch, especially not in my current mood. I raised one hand toward the flame, sucking in some of the fire pith. The flame sizzled to two-thirds of its original size.

Tabitha noticed immediately. She swirled to her right, then her left before she found me absorbing fire pith.

"What do you think you're doing, haggard?" she demanded, face furious and bathed in bonfire light.

"Helping another shepherd in a fight." I raised my chin in defiance. "Isn't that what we're supposed to do?"

Tabitha stomped toward me, halting in front of my face. Given our height difference, she towered over me. "This is training, not that you would recognize it," she hissed. "And you have no right to interfere."

I released all my anger at finding Vincent dating another woman. "I do if you're killing her!"

I expected some sort of reaction but not the intensity of what happened next. Her nostrils flared in her battle-hardened face as she upended the very ground beneath my feet, sending it flying upward in one swift strike. I flew up along with all that dirt, easily six feet off the ground. I didn't have the wits to soften the blow as I slammed down hard on my left side, debris half-burying me as it fell due to gravity.

Spitting out muck, I could only see Tabitha's toes as she spat out, "Don't you dare accuse me of harming my eyas!" Then, before I could stand, she manipulated the ground so that it shifted beneath me and rolled me away. I felt like I was on a conveyor belt made of muddy rolling pins as I spiraled helplessly along the upturned sod, my fingers unable to get a solid handhold anywhere.

Tabitha whisked me halfway across the field before finally relenting. In one final insult, she softened the ground to quicksand up to my waist so that I became stuck in the ground. By that time, I was yards away from the bonfire. I yelled at Tabitha's tiny stick figure in the distance, but she'd never let me loose. It took me fifteen minutes and a ton of earth sigils, but I eventually pulled myself out of the ground, covered in a thick layer of soil.

I could have gone back to the hot spring to clean, but I'd had about enough of today. The lodge stood not far off, so I stalked toward it, ready to fall asleep for a month.

I found out I wasn't alone inside the building. Azar boiled water for tea in the kitchen, stopping only for a second to give me a polite once-over before removing a kettle from the stone oven.

"Good eve, Ina," she said, not indicating she greeted a shepherd who looked like she had just lost a mud wrestling competition.

I mumbled something incoherent as I made my way to the pool area. I threw myself in, boots and all, not caring that dirt flaked off absolutely everywhere. It would all settle out quickly. Sipho had enchanted the entire lodge so it would stay clean no matter what we dragged in. Muddy particles detached from my clothes and slowly drifted up to the surface of the water, scooting toward the open floor, and finally spreading themselves out with the rest of the dirt. I floated on my back, clean again, and let out a long breath.

The kettle whistled and Azar poured herself a cup. "Would you like some too?"

My natural instinct was a sarcastic response, but I managed to bite it back. Dumping my frustration on Azar was unfair, and besides, she hadn't done anything to me. She was being polite. A distant kind of politeness, maybe, but it sure beat the derision I regularly received from the Sassy Squad.

"Sure," I answered.

Azar brought over a clay mug, placed it on the stones next to me, then moved to the other side of the pool to sit with her back to the fire, legs crossed beneath her. Rings of fire glistened in her dark hair as she took a few precise sips.

I couldn't help but ask, "Don't you want to know what happened to me?"

"I heard enough to hazard a guess." Her reply

held no judgment, a simple statement of fact.

But I wanted her to be judgmental. I hauled my butt out of the pool and unlaced my soggy boots. "Doesn't it bother you how hard Tabitha trains Darby?"

Azar did not so much as bat an eyelash. "Training strengthens the shepherd."

"And pain is just weakness leaving the body, right?" I threw my hands up in disgust. "It's really hard to toughen up if you're dead."

Azar maintained her matter-of-fact tone. "Tabitha would never allow another one of her eyases to perish. This I believe with all my spirit."

It took a second for that sentence to sink in. "Are you saying that Tabitha has lost an eyas before?"

That managed to crack Azar's emotional armor. She shifted slightly on her haunches, a little uncomfortable. "I merely state fact." I guessed by her stiff shoulders she wouldn't give me any more details.

My already heavy heart sank further. It seemed like the longer I stayed a shepherd, the more tragedy I encountered. "Guntram's told me about losing shepherds before. Is it common?"

"Common enough."

"Have you lost someone?"

"I have experienced the death of fellow shepherds, but I cannot feel it. Not the way normal shepherds do."

This stoic response took me aback. "Why not?"

Azar paused, choosing her words carefully.

"Like it or not, Nasci has given me a talent for fire. Fire allows for few emotions. Too much anger makes fire pith hard to control. Too much sadness weakens one's grip on it. If I am to become an augur as a fire shepherd, emotion is a luxury I can ill afford."

My mind reeled. How does someone repress their feelings so much they can't grieve? "That's bonkers. You'll go insane holding all that garbage in."

"Nevertheless, it is what I must do." She paused to give me a long, pointed stare. "It is something you might consider, Ina, shepherd of lightning. The only element I consider more erratic than fire is the electricity that lights the skies."

My face warmed. "You think I'm too hysterical to wield lightning?"

"Not at all," she said quickly. "I do not even know if emotions play a role with that element. We understand so little about lightning. Anything is possible."

"I hope it's not," I grumbled. "Because I can't stop feeling things. It's not in my nature at all."

Azar took a final sip from her cup. "Nasci only gives us gifts that we have the capacity to handle. She would not give you lightning if you did not have the inner strength to control it. But given its raw capacity, I doubt wielding it effectively will be easy."

I thought of Guntram taking me on all our lightning training excursions. I had a long way to go.

"So, what would you do, if you were me?"

Azar tilted her head thoughtfully. "Given lightning's rare and undocumented nature, you alone will be forced to discover this answer. It is a lonely path, even lonelier than fire. And if there is one thing I can guarantee from my own journey—" she paused as she stood, empty cup in hand, "—is that there is always a price to pay for our gifts. Deciding now that you are willing to pay that price will help bring you peace."

And on that cheery note, Azar wished me good night and retreated to her room.

CHAPTER 10

GUNTRAM RETURNED TO mentor mode at the crack of dawn the next morning. He smacked his fist on my door, threatening to douse me with water if I didn't get my hiney out of bed. It's not that I particularly enjoyed the straw-filled mattresses of the lodge (I didn't), but I did value sleeping in, something that Guntram and I never saw eye-to-eye about.

Guntram had laid out two very bland breakfasts of dry toast and tea, which would satisfy basic hunger but didn't make me jump for joy.

"You know," I said as I approached the counter bleary-eyed, "your racket could wake up Sipho's mountain lions."

"Everyone is awake save you, Ina. There's no need to be dramatic."

It didn't surprise me that everyone else was already awake, but glancing around the lodge, I thought I'd run into more people. I'd passed Darby tidying up her bedroom, but I hadn't seen hide nor hair of Tabitha or Azar.

"Where's everybody at?"

Guntram took a long sip from his cup, his signal that I should pay attention to what came next. "They're out on fire patrol."

I pushed back from the counter. "There's another fire?" I exclaimed louder than I meant to thanks to fuzzy morning brain. I lowered my voice a notch. "We don't have time for this nasty breakfast. We should get—"

"They're not evacuating the animals," Guntram cut me off. "They're simply on the watch for more fires in the area we protected yesterday."

This did not compute in my brain at all. Unlike the forest service, shepherds don't monitor for forest fires. They're a natural part of a forest ecosystem. We merely swooped in after the fact, save for one extreme example.

"You think there's another fire vaettur out there running amok?"

"The Oracle ordered it," Guntram said, as if this explained anything at all. "I sent Fechin to consult with her last night. She wants all of us to keep watch over the region for the next few days and note if other odd fires crop up."

"Why would there be more 'odd fires?' Correct me if I'm wrong, but vaetturs don't come in batches of elements like in some video game. Banishing one generally solves the problem."

Guntram folded his arms. "It's simply a precaution. There may be nothing to it at all."

I wanted to pull my hair out with all this vague crap. "Guntram, you gotta let me in here. First the bizarro breach, then the confused khalkotauroi acting like it had mad cow disease, and now we're suddenly on fire patrol 'just in case?'"

A new voice interjected into our conversation. "For once, can you accept an order without complaint?"

Darby entered the common area looking like I felt—dark circles under her eyes, limp hair, and rumpled cloak. While that may have been normal for me, Darby generally gave underwear models a run for their money. Finding her disheveled genuinely shocked me.

"Yikes, Darbs," I said without thinking.

Darby's nose turned up in disgust. "Not another word, haggard. After the little stunt you pulled last night, Tabitha put me through an additional hour of fire sigil training."

A twinge of guilt stirred in my gut. "Sorry."

"Next time, don't do me any favors." Darby plopped down on a stool next to me, eyeballing the second uneaten breakfast.

I nudged it toward her. "I didn't mean to get you in trouble."

She hesitated to touch the food now that I'd indicated I wanted her to have it. "Don't you live for trouble?"

"For myself, absolutely." I couldn't help but grin. "But not for others."

"You mean others like Jortur?" she snapped.

Ah, so she blamed me for the deer dryant's death too. She'd witnessed the whole terrible slaughter firsthand. Even though I wanted to be angry with her, I couldn't.

I decided on one last peace offering. "You know, Darby, I was really impressed with how you took on the khalkotauroi. You just stepped right up through the flames and faced it head-on. It was really impressive."

Guntram paused in between sips from his own cup to say, "Darby could be given her Shepherd Trial any day now. She has a solid mastery of all four elements under her belt."

"I can believe it after seeing some of it first-hand." I paused with self-reflection. "I always thought we were kind of neck-in-neck in abilities, but you've clearly pulled ahead."

Darby broke through my praise with a sneer. "Has it ever occurred to you that I've progressed because my augur pushes me to my limits? Because I've been at this longer? And that you might do well to take your own training more seriously?" She decided to emphasize her point by bumping my elbow, causing me to spill drops of tea on my hoodie.

"That's enough," Guntram said. "I'm tasked with escorting Darby to Tabitha's location this morning, and I will not tolerate bickering between the two of you. Is that clear?"

"Crystal," I said. For her part, Darby gave a curt nod.

Silence enveloped the room as Guntram finished packing supplies for the trip. I finished my own breakfast, and although Darby hesitated, she eventually went to town on the breakfast plate. It gave me the slightest glimmer of hope.

I guess I didn't completely ruin her appetite after all.

We remained quiet on the trip back to the Siuslaw National Forest. I used the time to wonder why we were going at all. Guntram loved to lecture that because shepherds never knew when a vaettur might appear, we always had to be prepared. I could not for the life of me figure out how the Oracle could possibly predict more vaettur-based forest fires.

We aimed for a rendezvous point with Tabitha near remote Pyle Creek. It turns out we weren't far from a clearcut logging operation. While we couldn't actually view it from our vantage point in the valley, you could hear the distinct sounds of machinery pushing over trees, beeping to back up, and generally crunching over everything in its wake. This kind of operation always puts a shepherd on edge, like listening to nails running down a chalkboard. Although mankind is technically a child of Nasci like all other animals, humans exploited nature for their own use way too often. That didn't exactly mesh with shepherd code.

Darby wrinkled her nose in disgust as we waited near a bend in the creek for Tabitha. "Humans. Such disgusting creatures."

I snorted. "You're one of them."

"Hardly." Darby tossed her hair behind one

shoulder. "I'm a shepherd, loyal to Nasci. The things over there—" she motioned toward the general direction of the noise, "—are as good as vaetturs, killing animals for their own personal gain."

I scoffed at this. "All forms of life depend on killing other forms in order to live. Heck, we even eat meat on occasion. Isn't that all part of the divine cycle?"

"Tearing down an entire forest isn't exactly in the spirit of the divine cycle," Darby countered. "How can there be balance when humans can reshape the entire world in their image, like a god?"

I mean, on one level, I agreed with her. As a shepherd, I hated how people did not value preserving a natural world untouched by their own hubris. And yet, shepherds hating regular people seemed like the height of hypocrisy. It's like when adults claim to hate children. I get that not everyone wants to have kids, but don't they realize they were once kids too? Isn't hating them kind of like hating yourself?

Tabitha arrived then, surrounded by a pair of black-tailed deer. Like the skittering bucks beside her, she grimaced at the sounds of the vehicles.

It put her in an even worse mood than normal. She dug right into Darby. "Are you finally recovered enough to do your job?"

I took a step forward to say something, but I remembered Darby's request to leave her alone. So I actually kept my lips zipped.

Darby proudly lifted her chin. "Ready."

Satisfied that her charge reacted appropriately to her demands, Tabitha then focused her attention on me. "Try not to mingle with your little friends back there." She pointed toward the source of the noise. "Remember the goddess you swore to serve."

I bristled at this accusation. "I'm as loyal to Nasci as any other shepherd."

Her eyes raked down my hoodie, shorts, and boots. "That remains to be seen."

Guntram grabbed my shoulder as the Sassy Squad flipped on their heels and disappeared into the trees. I hated that Tabitha got in the last word. Again. I waited until she left earshot before grumbling, "Who peed in her tea?"

Guntram motioned me in the opposite direction, away from the heavy machinery. "Come now, Ina. Despite your love of city life, you must understand why most shepherds find the general population an aggravation. You know the struggles we face with what few resources remain in the Talol Wilds."

"No, I get it. I really do. But even you don't think we should kill people, do you?"

"Of course not," Guntram replied quickly. "That's heresy. Shepherds do not kill creatures of Nasci without just cause."

"And admit it, you don't believe they're all bad. I noticed how you conveniently covered for Vincent during the debrief." I hated saying his name since I was still so angry at him, but I was also dying to understand Guntram's motivation. "Why did you do that?"

"I didn't cover for anyone," Guntram huffed into his beard. "Everything I said about him was completely accurate."

"But you've been mad at me for keeping in contact with him ever since the incident with the mishipeshu," I pressed. "And now, suddenly, you're cutting him some slack. Is it because he helped the owl and her nest?"

"I gave him the same courtesy I would bestow to any person who aided in the forest fire suppression," Guntram said. "We interfere as little as possible with humans, Ina. It's better that way, and you know it."

A flashback of Vincent driving away with his little girlfriend ran through my mind. "Yeah. It would be better if I never saw him again."

Guntram looked surprised that I agreed with him so easily. "Good. I'm glad you feel that way."

Guntram let the matter drop. We had our own area to scout. He led us south to Highway 36, a rather lonely country road that connects the major Oregon cities to the coast via a scenic, remote route. As we walked, Guntram taught me a basic fire suppression sigil—a trapezoid with a cross in the middle. Drawn on everyday objects like defensive sigils, Guntram explained that they wouldn't completely halt a fire, but they would keep flames from spreading as quickly. The sigils were only temporary, too, meaning they would only last a week or so.

We drew them every hundred yards or so on trees, rocks, even patches of dry ground. Breaking only for meals Guntram had packed for us, we put in a full day's work, never noticing anything outside of the ordinary. We reinforced a decent section from the town of Swisshome and ended up outside of Mapleton, traveling not far from the road.

We were beat when the sun set behind the mountains. Guntram decided we could quit for the day. We went through our normal camping routine: finding a quiet nook by a stream, lighting a fire, foraging for roots and berries, and locating the most comfortable spots to lie down for the night. A raccoon lumbered out of a bush to steal some berries I'd gathered for myself. Guntram's ravens did the same. I'd gotten used to nature's indigenous thieves a long time ago and had picked more food than I could eat so I could consume the amount I actually wanted.

It wasn't until the fire got low and my eyelids grew heavy that Guntram said, "Get some sleep, Ina. We've got a lot of ground to cover along Highway 126 tomorrow."

"Highway 126?" I asked in between a yawn. Unlike today's route, 126 was a major east-west road with lots of traffic. "What's with sticking around the highways, Guntram? Why don't we reinforce areas more toward the heart of the forest?"

"We have to start somewhere."

I didn't have the energy to argue. Sleep sounded too good. I let my sore body succumb to that numbness and fell asleep.

CHAPTER 11

IF YOU'VE NEVER lived around ravens, like I unfortunately have, then you don't know how freaking loud they are in the morning. Roosters don't have anything on ravens. Ravens flock in groups and screech their heads off as if the sun might not rise if they're not making enough racket to raise the dead.

That's why when I first heard Guntram's kidama uproar, I just groaned and pulled the top of my hoodie farther up over my head. My internal clock told me to ignore them. Unless Guntram started cawing at me too, I refused to crack my eyes open.

"Ina! Wake up!"

A sharp, stomach-turning scent assaulted my nose. It took me a few whiffs to realize it was smoke.

"Fire!" Guntram yelled.

I jolted awake. A distinctive red glow loomed out of the southwest. Half of Guntram's ravens had already taken off in that direction. I threw on my boots and followed Guntram, sprinting our way up, down, and around small hills to catch up to the blaze.

"The fire's breached where we drew sigils yester-day!" I screamed at Guntram's flying cape ahead.

Guntram called back over his shoulder. "That means the fire may be too strong for them. Stay sharp, Ina!"

A sense of foreboding came over me the far-ther we ran. We passed a familiar wisp channel, the trunk's base glowing with little blue firefly-like lights as we streamed past. I recognized the area. We were heading straight toward the geezer's farm where I'd withdrawn cash outside of Mapleton.

My worst fears were confirmed as we crested a hill and looked down at the fire. A burning inferno created a palm-shaped print below, one finger of fire streaking out toward a dilapidated shed. Be-yond it, the farmhouse squatted like a lamb in the grass. It would be only a matter of time before the fire destroyed the entire property.

Before I could point this out, Fechin flew down and landed on Guntram shoulder. Guntram grunted and nodded as they communicated tele-pathically. Then, in one swift beat, Fechin took back off into the sky.

"There's a herd of elk trapped over there." Gun-tram pointed on the opposite side of the blaze. "We must get them out."

My mouth went dry. "But what about the farm? Somebody lives there."

"The elk need us first. We'll swing back around to it if we have time."

I understood Guntram's priorities, so his decision didn't surprise me. Still, my heart pounded as the fire inched ever closer to the old man's house.

"We won't make it back in time!"

"We're shepherds, Ina. The elk come first." Guntram jogged down the hill. "Let's go."

I took a few hesitant steps behind Guntram, but I couldn't follow. The geezer may have pointed a gun at me, but he was still a flesh and blood person, living his life. I couldn't let him and his adorable dog burn to death.

I took a sharp left turn, angling down the other side of the hill. "I'll catch up to you!" I shouted behind me.

I thought I heard Guntram call after me, but kept pushing forward, tree trunks zipping by me like shadowy zombies underneath the blood red sky. The smoke actually thinned for several hundred yards, hanging above me, until I got closer to ground level and thus to the fire itself. I drew an octagon with a cross in the middle, providing me a straight path through the fire and toward my target much faster than circling around.

I'd barely taken a few steps out of the flames when Rufus the bullmastiff nearly plowed me over. I managed to maintain my balance while Rufus charged toward the house, ears flying backward like little black flags. He skittered on his paws until I caught up to him, barking and whining on the front porch.

"Good boy." I gave him a quick pat on the head.

He could have run off scared, and no one would blame him given the approaching fire, but he wanted to save his owner. Whoever said animals don't experience emotions didn't have half the morality of this pooch.

"Sir!" I banged on the door. "Sir!" But I knew he wouldn't respond, not if Rufus's barking had no effect on him. Was the geezer really that much of a sound sleeper?

I had no choice but to go inside the house. Remembering the geezer's shotgun, I grabbed onto the defensive charm hanging around my neck. It had saved me from a bullet before, and although it would hurt like hell, I trusted it would do so again. I tried the knob and found the door unlocked. I lurched inside.

And tripped over a groaning body.

I cursed as my knees slammed into the hard floor. I'd toppled over the geezer's bare bony legs, the rest of him (thankfully) covered in a long nightshirt. I opened my mouth to berate him for laying on the floor right inside the entrance when I noticed the gash on the side of his head. A trickle of blood matched a smear on the corner of a nearby side table. Not far from his slippered feet, a rug had been folded awkwardly in half. Scattered all around us were photos that had fallen out of an old shoe box.

The geezer must have slipped on his way out the door and hit his head.

I crawled over to him. "Sir! Can you hear me?"

He turned his head to the side. "Ouch. Tone it down, woman. I'm not deaf."

"I'm here to help." With only a little awkward maneuvering, I managed to get his arm around my shoulders and, ever so gingerly, helped him stand.

Once back on his feet, he wobbled unsteady, grabbing the doorframe.

"Can you walk?" I asked.

He blinked at me a few times. "Wait!" he cried. "Aren't you that punk that broke into my shed? What are you doing here?"

"Saving your sorry hide," I snapped back. "Now let's go!"

He grunted an affirmative, and I helped him out to the front porch, thankful that an excited Rufus jumped around us but not directly underfoot. That sense of relief fled as I caught sight of the shed, the backside having already caught fire. It wouldn't take long for that aging tinderbox to burst into high flames, fueling the fire toward this side of the yard.

We needed to leave. Now. I'm a shepherd of many talents, but even with endless earth pith at my disposal, I wouldn't be able to roll the geezer around the ground fast enough to keep ahead of the fire. And I didn't see any water anywhere for us to jump into. That left one last, non-magical option.

I eyeballed the only possibly working vehicle, the battered pick-up truck. "Does that thing run?"

"Better than you do," the geezer snarled. "And

it's twice as old."

Great. That really boosted my confidence. "Where are the keys?"

"In the cab."

"Then let's go."

The nasty old guy grabbed onto the porch railing, refusing to budge. "Not without my photos!"

"You've got to be kidding me!" I yelled. But I left him clutching the wooden poles as I marched back into the house. I grabbed overturned Polaroids by the handful, shoving them willy-nilly back into the shoe box. They all seemed roughly the same, taken in the 70s or 80s of some middle-aged woman that liked floral blouses, big hair, and thick black glasses. I marched back outside and showed the geezer the full box.

"Happy now?"

He grunted again. Shaking, he latched onto the crook of my arm and painstakingly navigated down the porch steps. I glanced over at the shed, completely up in smoke to its turquoise roof. The fire sizzled across the yellow grass toward us. The geezer started hacking as we shuffled as fast as he could manage across the lawn toward the pickup. I drew a quick infinity loop, two Ss joined mirror image, to create a spinning wind around us. It eased the smoke but wouldn't do diddly once the fire reached us.

When we got to the truck, I half-escorted, half-shoved the geezer into the passenger seat, then threw the box on his lap. Slamming the door, I raced to the driver's side, let Rufus slide in between us, then jumped in myself. The pick-up was so old it had cracked cloth seating with fluff sticking out everywhere across a bench seat, meaning if I wanted to scoot the driver's side up to the wheel (which, hello, I'm short), I had to scoot *all* of us forward—geezer, dog, and shepherd. I didn't have time for that, so I sat at the edge of the seat like a kindergartener, straining my right foot forward to find the gas pedal.

The fire had reached the front porch. I turned the key in the ignition and gave a shout in victory as the engine started on the first drive. Then, throwing it into reverse, I zoomed out of there, south on Highway 36.

I noticed the geezer bobbing up and down violently. "Put on your seat belt!" I cried.

But he didn't hear me, focused on the old house, fire slowly eating it alive. A tear leaked down his wrinkled face. "I'm so sorry, Millie," he muttered, clutching the shoe box to his nightshirt. "It's gone."

I swallowed a sudden lump in my throat. I wanted to say something comforting, like "Millie wants you to live" or "It's just a house," but given my verbal propensity for making matters worse, I kept my mouth shut. As we bumped down the gravel driveway and onto the (again thankfully) paved rural road, I tried to keep the ride smooth so he didn't die in a car accident while being rescued. I didn't think I could get him to fasten his seat belt in his current frame of mind.

We drove a few minutes in silence before I noticed a sign declaring Mapleton another three miles ahead. Finally, a break. Mapleton might be small, but even in the dead of night, there had to be some public place I could find help for the old man. I needed to drop him off and dart back into the forest. Guntram must have been furious with me by now.

We drove past a residential neighborhood on the west side of the Siuslaw River. I knew beyond the intersection of the two highways I'd find a few gas stations. I intended to drive there first until the distinctive strobe of emergency lights pierced the valley. Squinting, I could tell the source originated across the bridge, toward the center of town, although the houses along the river made it impossible to pinpoint any actual vehicles.

"I'm going to drive you over to those lights," I told the geezer. "They can get you to a hospital or something."

The geezer mumbled something, a faraway look in his eyes. At least he'd traded in crying for grumpiness. I handled the latter a lot better. Pulling into the left turn lane, I eased the pick-up truck across the bridge.

I expected a police car in a speed trap, making traffic cash for the local municipality. I did not expect a full fleet of cop cars, ambulances, and fire trucks crammed next to the combined middle and high school building. There were so many of them in the parking lot, several had spilled over into a carefully maintained grass field nearby. I parked the pick-up near these outliers.

"What in the hell is going on over there?" the geezer gaped out the windshield.

A decent crowd of people from adjacent houses had also gathered, most in their night clothes, necks craned to view the commotion. We both exited the pick-up, and I let the geezer lean on my arm so we could shuffle over to them.

A frazzled-haired woman carrying a fussy baby approached us. "Mr. Pitts!" she exclaimed, staring at the blood matted in his hair. "What happened to you?"

Her cries caused a decent chunk of the crowd to notice and offer aid. I gratefully allowed a middle-aged man in a stained tank top to take the geezer off my hands. They focused so intently on Mr. Pitts that they didn't see me back away. The less they questioned me, the better. I pinpointed a grove of trees that would allow me to melt back into the forest and inched my way in that direction. I wanted to know what was going on too, but I didn't have time. Mapleton would have to contend with its own problems.

I'd almost completely broken away from the crowd when a hand suddenly grabbed me by the elbow, pulling me backward.

"Hey!" I yelled, yanking my arm free.

I turned around to face striking blue eyes. My insult fell silent as I recognized the backpack and salon-tossed hair.

"Rafe?" I asked in surprise. "What are you doing here?"

"Ina, is it?" he greeted. "I could ask the same of you. Do you live here?"

"No." Then I realized his question answered one of my own. "But that means you don't live here either."

"I'm doing some research in the area," he explained. "What an odd coincidence, meeting again under such extreme circumstances. What brings you here?"

I blatantly ignored the question. He made it sound like he knew what the commotion at the school was about, so I focused on that. "What's going on?"

He stiffened. "Fire."

Fire? This far out? Fires spread fast, but the original blaze shouldn't have spread here from where Guntram and I saw it earlier. Unless...

My heart skipped a beat. Unless the vaettur that had started the fire had traveled this way.

"How did it start?" The words came out harsher than I intended, but I had to know.

Rafe raised an eyebrow but replied, "Back in the forest, I'm told, but spread this way by wind. The firefighters are spraying chemicals so it doesn't enter town."

His words confirmed my theory. There was likely a vaettur, possibly even another khalko-tauroi, somewhere out there starting fires. I had to stop it.

I dashed off into the trees without further explanation.

"Wait!" Rafe shouted after me.

I paid him no mind, grateful that I didn't hear him follow. The last thing I needed was some regular bro thinking he could save me, the damsel in distress. I was in distress, all right, and about to fling it right back in the face of the nasty monster that caused it.

I kept to the tree line, watching the firefighters hosing down the roofs of nearby houses with thick white foam. By the time I made it to the far end of the school yard, the temperature had risen, acidic smoke now thick in the wind.

And like a light switch coming on in a dark room, I sprinted right into a massive inferno.

It came on so suddenly, I'd only half prepared for it. I choked as I drew a quick cross with an octagon, trying my best to force fire pith to flow through my pithways rather than my lungs. As my anxiety rose, I struggled to maintain balance, standing in the flames. I recalled Azar's words, how mastering fire meant letting go of all emotion. I closed my eyes on the molten terrorscape before me, taking deep breaths and telling myself everything would be okay. Everything would be okay.

Then I opened my eyes to a vaguely humanoid shape punching me to the ground.

All intentions of serenity fled in the wake of

the attack. I dodged a second fist to the chin but received a kick to my side for my efforts, throwing me back into the ashes. My internal temperature rose dangerously. I grabbed my water charm, drawing a series of Vs with a slash through them. A steaming current of water whipped out of my fingertips, directed at my attacker.

The figure screamed, a mixture of a real cry and crackling fire, as it shielded itself with its arms from my attack. It was then I got my first good glance at the thing. Definitely not a bull, and certainly not any animal I'd ever seen. Instead, it appeared as the shadow of a man made completely of fire, standing several feet taller than me, with no real physical form underneath that I could tell. It had no distinguishable hands or feet, just stumps, as if someone had cut them off at the ankles and wrists. As it turned to me in hate, I noticed it had no real eyes or mouth, only gaping cavities of intense fire that burned where those features should have been.

It didn't appear or act like any vaettur I had ever fought. It looked more like a demon straight out of hell.

My water charm's pith ran out of juice, so I drew on the rest of my inner reserves. As I drew a five-pointed star, I sneered at the fire demon.

"Bye, bye!" I yelled as I let the water banishment sigil fly.

Now, I know that not all banishment sigils work as effectively against all vaetturs. A fire vaettur isn't necessarily weak to water, even though it's not a bad bet. Still, even if a banishment doesn't outright get rid of the little suckers, it usually causes them some pain. I was trying to fling him back to his home world through a tear in space-time. It's not supposed to tickle.

But this thing, whatever it was, didn't so much as blink as water pith struck it square in the chest. In fact, the attack meant so little to the demon that it charged straight forward without pause, arms blazing like scorching baseball bats of death.

The thing wanted me dead. I didn't have a lot of coherent thought at that point, except dying wasn't high on my to-do list. When you're face-to-face with impending doom, you grab your biggest boomstick to fight it off. My fingers clutched the metallic cylinder around my neck crammed with four batteries' worth of lightning pith. I sucked the entire charm's storage of pith, then focused it in a lightning banishment on my enemy. As it surged out of my arm, it made my whole body go numb.

Normally, when I release lightning, it packs a pretty powerful punch. It's hard to control, but I generally can at least fling it in some general direction, even if I can't really aim it.

Not so with Sipho's lightning pith charm.

The lightning bolt that shot out of my hand burst in all directions like a bomb. It had an intensity to it I'd never released before. It made the forest fire around us fade into bright shadows. The entire world went a stark white, engulfing the surprised fire demon. It also created a sonic boom that probably left people deaf for miles.

It was within that sightless and soundless space that I fell unconscious, having busted straight past the limits of what I could handle.

CHAPTER 12

I WOKE UP in a hospital room.

At first, the setting didn't register in my muddled brain. I smelled the disinfectant, coarse linen sheet pulled up to my chest, harsh fluorescent light bulbs clashing with the natural sunlight attempting to stream in between the vertical window blinds. A beeping on a machine next to me reassured me I had a pulse. But I didn't bring all those sensations together until I saw a blonde-haired pretty boy slumped over in the world's least comfortable armchair, fast asleep. He wore the same outdoor clothing as before, a backpack crumpled at his feet.

"Rafe?" I croaked.

Memories came flooding back in a rush—the fire, saving the geezer, running into Rafe outside of the school, and facing the weird fire demon. The last thing I remember was going guns out in a spectacular lightning blast, and then fade to white. End scene.

Rafe must have heard me because he stirred in his seat. A red mark remained on his cheek where his shoulder had dug into the flesh too long, but even that somehow made him appear cute. He flashed me a comforting smile.

"Good morning, Ina."

"Morning?" It had been the middle of the night only seconds ago, but sure enough, the annoying ticking clock on the wall read ten. "What's going on?"

"You're in a hospital. Don't worry, everything's okay."

I didn't want to rehash stuff I already knew. "Yeah, I got that part. I mean, what brought me here?"

"The firefighters found you in the middle of a charred section of forest, unconscious but alive. They brought you here."

I wish they hadn't. The hospital couldn't do anything for me that an hour at the hot spring wouldn't fix. But I had other problems to deal with. "And the fire? Did they contain it?"

"I think so," Rafe shrugged.

I leaned back into my pillow, relaxing a smidge. I guess that meant I'd actually gotten rid of that weird fire demon. I couldn't believe it had attacked so close to civilization in the first place. I doubted it would have simply walked away and stopped setting fires unless I'd blasted it back where it came from.

Nothing about that thing felt normal.

Rafe scooted his chair closer so he could place one hand on the hospital bed railing. "But more importantly, I'm glad you're okay."

I blushed in spite of myself. People don't gush over me. They roll their eyes, give me unwanted advice, and berate my decisions, but besides Vincent, they didn't generate a ton of genuine concern for me.

I shouldn't have thought of Vincent. My blush morphed into a scowl. I hated how that awful sting of jealousy reared its head when his memory popped up. How my heart ached. Hadn't I left teenage crushes behind a long time ago?

Rafe noticed my mood shift. "Is something wrong?"

"No, I'm just groggy. It happens when you run headfirst into fire."

"I suppose that's not something ordinary people can relate to." He pinned me down with those gorgeous eyes. "Only something a shepherd can do."

The startled gasp left my lips before I could stop it. It made my next shaky sentence much less believable. "What are you talking about?"

Rafe threw me a conspiratorial smirk. "Come now, Ina. You know exactly what I'm talking about. You relied on your fire pith to walk through that blaze. No other explanation makes sense."

I sat up in the bed, every muscle clenched. How could he know all this stuff? "Who are you?"

He raised a palm in friendly surrender. "Not an enemy, I assure you. Quite the opposite. An ally of the shepherds, actually, even if they don't want my help."

I had never heard of anyone outside of our world talk about shepherds. Even Vincent, who eventually accepted me for what I was, had never heard of anything like us. "I don't understand."

Rafe stood up to his full height, fervent with his next words. "There are followers of Nasci outside of your circle, Ina. People who believe passionately that we must stop harm to her at all costs. But alas," he adopted a solemn, almost angry tone, "not all of us can harness elemental pith the way you can. We have to rely on other methods to do our part."

"Other methods?" My mind could barely keep up with this surreal conversation.

"Have you ever heard that vaetturs possess their own kind of pith?"

I balked at that. "Vaetturs devour Nasci's pith."

"That's true, of course, but have you ever wondered how it is that they often wield the same elements as shepherds? Earth, water, air, even the latest one, the copper bull, burned with flame?"

"You know about the khalkotauroi?" This conversation just kept getting more bizarre.

Rafe nodded. "That's how I ran into you when we first met. I was tracking the bull. Even then, I suspected you might be a shepherd. You appeared near a breach in the middle of nowhere with no real means of transportation. When you responded to the raven's call—" he stiffened slightly, "—I knew you must be a shepherd."

My brain jammed, processing all this information. I decided to stick to one detail at a time. "So, if you were tracking the bull, does that mean you were trying to banish it too?"

"Not banish it, use it," Rafe said. "Suck out its fire pith and let the vaettur wither and die, like the way they kill dryants."

"That's crazy!" I cried. "Shepherds don't kill vaetturs, we send them back to Letum. It's unheard of to do anything else."

"Only unheard of because it's shepherd tradition," Rafe argued. "But given what I've witnessed of you, Ina, you're not one to adhere to tradition, are you?"

My voice rose a notch. "And what exactly do you think you know about me?"

"I know you can absorb lightning pith."

The blood drained from my face.

He nodded, acknowledging my surprise. "Oh yes, I understand how rare it is to be able to do that. But that lightning strike confirmed it. It scared the daylights out of all of us watching at the school."

"It was just a random lightning bolt," I mumbled. "It happens."

"Without a single cloud in the sky?" Rafe chuckled. "No, that was Nasci, the work of a shepherd." He sat back down. "But I get why you would deny it. Trust me, I know all about how strict shepherd life can be. The others probably fear you. Resent you. See you as a threat. You break the rules, merely by your very existence."

He really didn't know the half of it. "Okay, so

you know a lot about shepherds," I said, wanting to steer the conversation away from my unique abilities. "Then why are you here, watching me unconscious in a hospital bed like a creeper?"

"Because I recognize an opportunity for someone like me to assist someone like you. To prove that more people than shepherds can worship Nasci and protect her from harm."

I didn't have time to respond to this theatrical proposal as footsteps approached the hospital room.

"Ina," Vincent called, breathless as he rounded the corner. "I heard about a woman with no ID being brought here from a fire call last night. You matched the description, so I came here as soon as..." He trailed off as he caught sight of Rafe. All hint of worry left his voice, replaced by a brusque, "Oh."

Rafe bowed his head slightly. "I was about to leave," he drawled. He reached into his backpack and pulled out a light gray stone with tiny hairline cracks, the ubiquitous kind you find all around the woods. He placed it gently on my palm.

"We'll find each other when you're ready to test the waters," he whispered in my ear, then closed my fingers around the stone. A shiver went up my spine as his caress lingered on my skin. Then he hoisted the backpack over his shoulder and exited the room.

Vincent's lips went so tight, I thought he'd sucked them straight down his throat. He stared at my hand holding the stone.

"Who was that?" he demanded.

I shifted the hand out of sight underneath a blanket. "Somebody I met in the woods. He was at the fire last night."

"He's not a firefighter. I know that crew." He frowned at the doorway. "And he doesn't look like a local."

"He's just a hiker. He's harmless."

But Vincent wouldn't let it go. "Not all hikers are harmless, Ina. I've met some really dangerous people lurking in the woods. Violent. They live out there to escape society. Or prey on it. If I were you, I'd steer clear of that guy."

I couldn't believe Vincent of all people had waltzed into the room to tell me who I should and should not hang out with.

"Excuse me, but it's none of your business," I said curtly.

"I thought we were friends," Vincent threw back, his anger mounting. "How do you think I felt when I heard you'd been injured in the fire last night?"

His declaration of so-called concern snapped my composure in half. "It probably feels about as terrible as when you waltz into a random bar and find a guy you nearly kissed on a date with his side piece."

Vincent flinched at the vehemence in my voice. "What are you talking about?"

"I'm talking about the pub in Eugene, Garcia. I

was there. I saw you drive off with your girlfriend. Don't play dumb with me."

I wanted Vincent to deny it. I wanted him to tell me I couldn't believe my own eyes, even though I still wouldn't believe him.

But instead, he said, "You were there?"

I'd had my fill of this hospital and all the obnoxious conversations associated with it. I yanked the IV out of my arm, causing the machine to curse at me as well. This only set me off further.

"Yes. I was at the bar, Vincent, so don't come waltzing in here telling me how much you care about me when you're banging some other chick in Eugene."

I grabbed the pile of my clothes they'd left on a vacant chair, balanced the boots on top, and shoved the weird stone Rafe gave me into a pocket. Vincent tried to block the door as I made to leave.

"It's not like that, Ina. We're not a thing."

My fire pith rose to my fingertips even before I raised my hands. "You're not going to be a thing in about two seconds if you don't get out of my way."

Vincent wisely stepped to the side but followed me as I stalked down the hallway. "Ina, you're being unreasonable. They're not going to let you walk out the front door without an official release."

I glanced down the long hallway, past the nurses' station and out toward the automatic sliding glass doors, where an aging security guard stood by.

I flipped on my heels and spotted the barred emergency exit. "Then I'll find another way out."

Vincent realized my plan as I took off at a full sprint. "What? No!" he cried. "Wait!"

The piercing wail of the emergency door's siren blocked out all other protest. I didn't slow down as I ran across the parking lot, pebbles digging into my bare feet. They didn't sting nearly as much as the tears as I fled toward the wisp channel that would take me far away.

CHAPTER 13

I SHOULD HAVE gone straight back into the Siu-slaw to find Guntram to let him know I was okay, but since I'd gotten rid of that fire demon thing, no one was in any real danger. Besides, my body jiggled like loosely functioning spaghetti. Physically, the hospital had done zero to alleviate the pain from electrifying myself into unconsciousness. Mentally, I could barely keep myself from full out crying, overwhelmed by both men's dramatic conversations at the hospital. So instead of being a responsible shepherd, I hightailed it back to Sipho's and marched straight to the hot spring.

Soaking in waters fed by magma, Nasci's lifeblood, acted like a soothing balm. All the pith oozed out of my pores, a kind of osmosis flowing between me and the high levels of energy contained in the spring water itself. I closed my eyes and allowed the sensation to rock me like a mother and child, rhythmic, back and forth.

It didn't solve anything, of course. I still felt betrayed by Vincent, who hadn't even bothered denying meeting this girl of his. The way they had acted together, they had to share some deep history. And I'd noticed that brief flash of guilt on his face when I confronted him, like he'd been caught in some way.

I clenched my hands into fists under the water. How could I have been so dumb?

And to make matters worse, now I had Rafe to contend with as well. Another outsider who had taken an interest in me. But he was more unusual than Vincent. Rafe not only knew way more about shepherds than any normal person should, he thought he could help us. This flew in the face of everything Guntram had taught me about becoming a follower of Nasci. Only the chosen few heard the goddess's call, and only they could take on the sacred task of protecting Nasci's precious life energy flowing through every living being on this planet.

"Fool me twice," I whispered. I couldn't fall into the trap of trusting strangers again. Not after what doing so with Vincent had taught me.

But why did making that resolution leave me feeling so empty?

I became so lost in my own thoughts that I didn't hear Sipho walk down the stone steps to the first pool. "Ina!" she exclaimed. "What are you doing back by yourself?"

I glanced upward and quickly glanced away. Sipho had already removed all her clothes and wore nothing. Sunlight filtering through the trees hit her bare skin, glistening with sweat. She must have just finished some hard, physical labor, not surprising given the kind of work it took to keep the homestead in tip-top shape.

"I ran into some trouble," I told my hands as she sank down into the water on the other side of the pool. I looked up at her again once she'd covered herself from the breasts down. "I needed a quick recharge before heading back out."

Sipho's gaze lingered on my collarbone. She frowned. "I can see that. You not only broke your lightning charm, but your defensive charm shattered too."

My fingers brushed up against my charm necklace, and sure enough, both aforementioned charms had jagged edges, the etchings of them broken so they no longer served their primary function. I hadn't even noticed it, since the necklace had been the one thing the hospital had never removed from my body.

I threw her a wry smile. "I'll give you one guess how using the lightning charm went."

Sipho's eyes widened slightly. "That's how you broke the defensive charm?"

I nodded.

She cursed under her breath. Then she scooted closer and held her hand out to me. "I worried about such a possibility. Can you give me a detailed description of what happened when you drew lightning from the charm?"

After sliding the twisted metal off my neck, I gave her a recap of the explosion I'd caused fighting the fire demon—how I couldn't control the lightning, its ridiculous intensity, and the bolt knocking me out cold.

She twisted the charm up in the air, scrutinizing it first with her right eye, then her left. "The pith did not flow the way I expected it too. It appears to have swelled in places it should have pooled, and vice versa."

Sipho often talked about the ebbing and flowing of pith. I sort of understand it, since my own pithways have a rhythm to them, but how she could predict within the confines of an inanimate object how pith should react always blew my mind.

It made me curious about other things she might know about. "Sipho?" I asked slowly. "Have you ever heard of people outside of the followers of Nasci who worship her? Who want to help us?"

Sipho glanced at me in alarm. "No," she said sharply. "Why? Did your augur mention something of this nature?"

"No," I said, a little irritated at how quickly my line of reasoning had been blocked. "I haven't had a chance to ask him about it yet."

"Haven't had a chance?" she repeated, confused. "Doesn't Guntram know where you are?"

"No," I admitted, careful not to give away too many details.

Sipho gasped. "If Guntram does not know where you are, you should go to him immediately."

The thought of hauling my sore carcass out of the hot spring after such a short recharge made me groan. "I don't know what use I'll be in this condition."

"You should let Guntram decide," she insisted, shooing me toward my soiled hoodie and shorts in a pile on the rocks behind me. "Go on. Get dressed and find him. Can you find the way back to his general vicinity? I could send Nur with you to help track him, if necessary."

I knew I wasn't getting out of this. "Yeah, yeah," I grumbled, pulling myself fully out of the water. I drew a quick sigil to instantly dry myself. No need for towels when you can manipulate water. "I'll be fine without the kitty escort."

I threw on my clothes and had hauled my sorry flesh halfway up the steps when Sipho called to my back, "Don't forget to drop by the forge and pick up a new defensive charm. It may come in handy."

I had no idea at the time how true that would really be.

CHAPTER 14

LOCATING GUNTRAM IN the thousand square miles of the Siuslaw National Forest would be no easy task. If he stuck around Mapleton, where I'd last seen him, it would narrow things down a bit. Yet, as I navigated through a rapid series of wisp channels pushing me farther toward the coast, I wondered exactly how I would find him. I didn't have kidama ravens to send messages for me, nor did I have any idea where that herd of elk might have relocated.

As it turned out, all I needed was my sense of smell.

A few miles past Mapleton, deep in the woods, I caught a whiff of smoke. It jolted me to attention. Azar had banished the khalkotauroi, and I'd gotten rid of the fire demon. It was weird enough to encounter two powerful fire vaetturs in a row. There couldn't possibly be another one on the loose.

Could there?

If there was anything I'd learned over the last few months as a shepherd, though, once you had certain expectations, something would smash them to pieces. I scaled a nearby mountain cliff, drawing a square with a triangle with my earth pith to allow my exposed fingertips to stick to the rock wall, making the climb easier. When I finally summited the top, my already whimpering muscles went into full-blown howling mode.

"This had better be worth it," I grumbled as I scanned the rolling treetops.

A towering belch of black smoke arched up from behind a mountain on the other side of a small valley.

Great. I wished I had Guntram's ridiculous air abilities and could force a stream of wind under my feet so I could glide over the distance. But I knew I'd probably land somewhere below with broken legs if I attempted such an advanced maneuver.

So I ran.

I took off down the mountainside, letting gravity pull me ever faster as I sprinted at a steep angle toward the creek at the bottom of the valley. I vaulted over the rocky shores, barely wetting my boots as I dashed back uphill at a much slower clip. Dodging foliage and sometimes scrambling on logs for balance, I made it to the next crest relatively quickly. I expected to find a decent swatch of trees on fire.

I did not expect the world's largest bonfire burning inside a logging operation.

I'd stumbled across a clearcut patch of earth, this one much larger than the one near the khalkotauroi. It hurt my heart to see so many mammoth logging vehicles with talon-like claws, sawing blades, and bulging truck beds surrounding a gigantic pyramid made of generations of trees. Worse still to view that all ablaze, the logs green and wet on the inside, but their outer rims burning from our uncharacteristically dry spring. The cloud of smoke it made rose above the surrounding forest, giving off the ironic scent of pine and death.

And the cherry on top was the fire demon I'd thought I'd banished, more than twice as tall as before. It cackled with sizzling breath, waving its stumpy arms toward the blaze.

I cursed. So much for lightning getting rid of this thing.

Before I could move, I heard screams approaching rapidly up the mountainside. I crouched behind a bush just as a group of loggers in orange vests and hard hats came running past. One of them, the foreman by the black brick radio he carried in his hand, paused to wave all the others ahead. He brought the radio to his lips and yelled into it but received only static on the other end.

"We can't contact HQ!" he yelled at the men. "Keep going! We'll try again at the next ridge!"

Then he took the caboose and vanished with the rest of the loggers retreating into the forest.

I waited until I could no longer hear them before coming out of my hiding place. Apparently, the demon had interrupted a busy workday. This was nuts. The attack so close to Mapleton had been bizarre on its own, but I had never heard of vaetturs attacking humans directly. What was going wrong with the world?

I jogged down to the construction site, keeping inside the tree line and hoping to assess the situation before determining what to do. Near the edge of the clearing, a flurry of movement caught my attention. Behind the demon and the smoke, a skulking figure with platinum flowing hair snuck toward the demon. Darby. She dodged in between the machinery not far away, still out of the demon's sight. She put her back against a vehicle's boom, closed her eyes as if in prayer, and then, with a deep breath, her fingers flew as she generated a water shield as a defense.

"Oh no, Darbs," I whispered. "You're not taking that thing on alone, are you?"

But she did. In one fluid leap, she bounded toward the fire demon, water whipping toward her target in an attack. The demon spotted her immediately, sending up a wall of fire that absorbed most of the spray. Then the fire demon roared at her, flat legs pounding the ground as she retreated, but it was no use. The demon followed her, sending fireballs in her direction even as she ducked into a harvester cab. The vehicle's window sustained a blast of fire, spiderweb cracks fracturing the surface.

She was trapped.

I jumped into the clearing, racing toward them.

Darby might have been on the verge of full shep-herdom, but I'd fought this monster before. She launched a second stream of water at the demon from around the cab, but I knew water wouldn't hurt it. Sure enough, the demon broke through Darby's stream without so much as slowing down. Darby's eyes widened in terror when she realized she'd locked herself into a corner.

I latched onto my earth charm and, with my free hand, drew a square with a single slash under-neath it. I let my entire stash of earth pith flow from my charm, through one arm and out the other. I flung it in between the fire demon and Darby, praying I would make it.

The dirt wall that shot up in front of the har-vester slashed right through the demon's extended fiery arm. It cut a few feet off as its fluid body slammed into the earth wall. The demon lost its shape in a fiery burst, but its momentum slammed into the solid dirt wall, which toppled. Rocks threatened to crush Darby in the cab.

"Look out!" I yelled, hoping my voice would carry over to Darby. I didn't have time for a sec-ond sigil as huge boulders rained down on the har-vester.

Darby, though, had earth chops in spades. She drew a rapid set of square sigils I didn't recognize. The rock exploded into dust, spreading out in a fine powder over the vehicle. I coughed as particles shot up my nose, coated my mouth, and even pene-trated my lungs. I pushed forward anyway, creating an air bubble around my face in order to find my comrade in the rocky mist.

"Darby!" I screamed. "Where are you?"

After a few heart-stopping beats, someone sputtered on my right. I shot forward and found Darby on the ground, near the comically large tire of the harvester, covered in so much dust she looked like she'd just walked through an erupting volcano.

I cried out as I kneeled beside her. "Are you okay?"

She sputtered something into the ground, unable to form a coherent sentence.

I created a clean pocket of air for her as well. "Sorry about the mess," I said as she hacked away into the crook of her arm. "I didn't mean to gas you."

"Need..." she wheezed, "distraction."

"Distraction?"

She pointed over my shoulder, and I tracked her finger. The fire demon was nowhere to be found, but the blaze he had set in the logs continued to burn, somehow even taller than before. I cringed, wondering if the astronauts on the International Space Station could see it burning.

I drew a sigil for a ball of water, letting all my water pith pool to my palm. "It's a bigun for sure, but we can stop the fire before it spreads," I promised Darby.

But she shook her head violently. "No!" she cried. "Distraction!"

And that's when Satan's fiery BFF reformed. It

built itself from the ground up, a small ball of fire enlarging like a balloon. As it developed limbs and fathomless glowing eyes, I knew we were truly screwed. It towered so high over us, it obscured the bonfire of logs behind it.

Then it drew its long arm and smacked a crane holding a fresh batch of trunks. It knocked one large caber loose, which came barreling toward us.

My muscles tightened as I spread both arms over a prone Darby, unable to defend herself. I took the brunt of the falling log, its curved side smacking me in the back. It hurt like hell as it hit my invisible defensive barrier, but fortunately the charm took the brunt of the impact. I would survive. The thin metal slat, however, did not, shattering into glittering metal splinters.

I no longer had any passive protection.

The demon snapped its arm back for a second strike on the crane, hoping to rain more logs on our heads.

An echo of Rafe's conversation echoed in my brain. *Suck out its fire pith and let the vaettur wither and die.*

Backed into a corner and on the verge of getting pummeled to death, I would have tried anything. I turned away from a coughing Darby and raised my hands, palms out, to absorb pith directly from the demon.

It was a mistake.

Sharp pains ratcheted up and down my arms, as if my blood had solidified into a honey-like consistency but still tried to flow. The sensation spread quickly to my core, overwhelming all the other pith I had stored. I tried to breathe but couldn't, gasping for air like a fish. It almost knocked me unconscious. I closed my eyes to re-focus my mind.

But then the vaettur pith flow suddenly ceased.

A garbled cry of dismay filled my ear drums. Released from that terrifying energy I'd tried to absorb, I cracked an eye open to find the fire demon hovering right over us, limb ready to strike. By all accounts, it had us dead to rights, leaning in, my face only inches away from it. But instead it had stopped its assault.

Probably because its body had begun to fade.

Like messing with contrast on a screen, the fire demon lost its vibrant bright orange licks of flame, slowly melting into a shapeless white. Wisps of smoke seemed to pull the demon backward, from its elbows, knees, and head. It shrank, withering like a snowball left out in the sun, slow but inevitable.

As it diminished to only a few feet in height, the huge bonfire behind it reemerged into view. And that's when I saw the other shepherds. Guntram, Tabitha, and Azar all stood at odd angles on lit logs in the dead center of that flame, their bodies emitting a strange glow although they remained untouched by the inferno around them. Azar stood in the center, the focal point of their magic, her red bracelet glowing almost white hot with heat. The three shepherds executed a series of sigils that I recognized as fire-based but had never seen before. A line of fire surged from the augurs straight into Azar, whose sigils siphoned the very essence of fire straight off the demon.

They were sucking the fire right out of their enemy.

The fire demon retained its humanoid shape right up until it stood only a foot tall. Then, almost like a crying baby doll, it vanished forever, having been sucked into the very blaze it had created.

CHAPTER 15

WE RETURNED AS a group to the homestead, completely wiped out. Even Tabitha looked like she'd been wrung out like a wet rag. No one even bothered to go to the lodge this time. As daylight threatened to give way to night, everyone headed for the hot spring, a pathetic group of battle-weary shepherds.

I mean, I totally understood why. After touching the pith from that awful thing, I felt like someone had taken a steamroller over me, then tazed me for good measure. I needed a recharge as much as everyone else who'd fought the fire demon.

And yet, I couldn't keep my mouth shut. I grabbed Guntram by the arm. "So that's it?" I asked him, trying to keep my voice down so only he could hear. "No debrief, no nothing. Just welcome home and forget the whole thing."

Tabitha, unfortunately, had the hearing of one of her deer kidama. She turned on me. "You should be grateful to be back, haggard, after the stunt you pulled."

I had no patience left for Tabitha's lippy attitude. "Grateful that I saved Darby? Sure, you're welcome."

Tabitha bristled. "You did not save anyone. Darby was executing a distraction so we could mount an attack to defeat the beast. She would have done a fine job without you."

I opened my mouth to protest but got some completely unexpected back-up. "No, Tabitha," Darby cut in softly. "Ina did save me."

This halted Azar as well, who up until this point had avoided the group's bickering. "Come again?"

Darby straightened. "The vaettur had me trapped inside a metal machine. If not for Ina's intervention, it might have killed me before you could finish your work."

"I saw none of this!" Tabitha objected.

"You wouldn't have," I shot back. "That thing stood like a solid wall between you and us. Unless you can tell me you have some divine power to see through things, then I suggest you back off."

Tabitha reddened at my harsh tone.

Darby paled. "I'm sorry, augur. You told me to always tell the truth."

Uh oh. I wondered how many miles Darby would have to run tonight now that I'd shot off my mouth.

But Tabitha relaxed. She scooted over to brush Darby's hair. "I am grateful for your honesty, always. Even more grateful that you're alive." She still looked like she wanted to strangle me, but she settled on pretending I didn't exist. "Come, Darby.

Let's heal. Tomorrow will be another day for training."

You could have knocked me over with the slightest wind gust. Tabitha not laying into me was akin to an apology, and she wasn't even going to punish Darby for it.

Darby glanced back at me once as the Sassy Squad sauntered away. She nodded at me, which I didn't know how to interpret. Relief? Thanks? Or a begrudging warning to stay back? I didn't have an advanced enough degree in psychology to figure it out.

Azar made a motion to follow but paused to cock her head at me, a frown on her face. "And how about you, Ina? Will you join us at the hot spring?"

Guntram answered for me. "We have some things to discuss. Privately."

Ah, there it was. Tabitha might spare me but not Guntram. I geared myself up for the inevitable shout fest.

Given Azar's cool nature, I'd thought she'd steer clear of this kind of conflict, but she surprised both of us by saying, "Are you sure she shouldn't soak first?" She stared at me pointedly.

"I'm fine," I lied. "I actually got a dip in the springs before the fight."

"If you say so. It's just that something feels..." she let her sentence drift off, shaking her head. "Be well, Ina, and replenish yourself when you can."

Then Azar walked away.

Guntram waited until Azar had walked well out

of earshot before rounding on me. "That's where you were? Taking a break here at Sipho's while I searched the forest for you, believing you dead?"

I threw my hands up in the air. "C'mon, Guntram. It's more complicated than that."

"It's always complicated with you. You had no business running off when we had real shepherd duties to attend to."

"I saved a man and a dog from becoming burn victims," I said through gritted teeth. "Wasn't that our job?"

Guntram folded his arms. "The elk should have taken precedence, and you know it. Without my aid leading them through the fire, they would have died too."

"But they didn't die, did they?" I countered in triumph. "You did it all on your own. I saved creatures, you saved creatures, so why am I being read the riot act?"

"Because of shepherd code, Ina!" Guntram snapped, his face red. "We protect animals over people. Humans can take care of themselves. Nasci knows they've torn the forest to shreds with their wretched greed."

I attempted reason. "I get why you're mad at people in general, but think about what you're saying. Do you really think even though there were two of us, and we both managed to save creatures of Nasci, that I'm the one in the wrong here? I should have let that geezer and his dog die because of what? A sense of priorities?"

Guntram rubbed his temples, clearly conflicted. "You couldn't have known at the time whether we could have saved them both."

A mirthless laugh escaped my lips. "Don't try to pull the whole 'you're too inexperienced' line on me. It's getting old."

Guntram's jaw tightened. "What are you talking about?"

"I'm talking about all the secrecy regarding these fires. Like how you guys were certain that another, different vaettur would attack after the khalkotauroi. How you never addressed how strange the khalkotauroi acted in the first place, acting like it was high on drugs."

Guntram blew his top at this line of reasoning. "You run off in the middle of a banishment to go take a dip in the hot spring, and you have the audacity to wonder why you aren't privy to confidential information?"

"I didn't run off," I protested. "I was knocked out."

Whoops. I knew I shouldn't have mentioned that little fact when Guntram's face managed to grow darker. But the truth had already slipped out. I forged ahead. "That's right. I met up with the fire demon and fried it with an electric banishment, but it knocked me out cold. A bunch of firefighters took me to the hospital. I got out as soon as I could, but I thought I'd taken care of our little friend until we met up again in the woods." As the words came out of my mouth, a strange realization hit me.

Guntram plowed ahead before I could verbalize it. "You exposed yourself to more people? Did they see you cast the banishment?"

"No, they didn't see anything. But Guntram," I rounded on him, more scared than defiant now. "How did you do it?"

He didn't follow my broken train of thought. "What are you babbling about?"

"The fire demon. You didn't banish it. You sucked it dry." I stared at him. "That's not how we're supposed to get rid of vaetturs."

I wanted him to respond with some sort of reassurance, that by performing those sigils, he and the others hadn't broken a supposed sacred tenant that we'd honored ever since I became a shepherd.

You banished vaetturs. That's the only way to send them back to Letum. You never absorbed them.

Rather than soothing my fears, Guntram became more flustered. "There are things you don't understand out there, Ina."

My aches from the fire demon battles throbbed enough that I didn't care anymore. I grabbed Guntram by the tunic collar. "Was that thing even a vaettur?"

Guntram pushed me backward, and I fell to the ground. He'd always been a grumpy old man but now he rose above me as an angry sorcerer, someone not to be crossed.

"You will not demand answers from me!" he yelled, his ravens taking off from the trees to create a flying circle above his head, cawing in agitation. "You are my eyas, and you will act like it, or so help me, I will bind you myself!"

I cowered for the first time ever in his presence. I did not recognize this person, so full of vehemence and violence.

"Do I make myself clear?"

I could only nod.

Guntram visibly shrunk at my immediate acceptance. His eyebrows softened, making him appear more sad than angry. Then he flipped on his heels and stormed off, more ravens joining his disjointed flock as he made his way not toward the hot spring but the library.

CHAPTER 16

I HAD NO idea how to process Guntram's anger. He'd been mad at me before but never like that. I hoped a good night's rest might reset our moods. I even woke up only an hour after dawn to start my day. I hoped my luck had changed when the only symptom left from absorbing that creepy vaettur pith was a mild headache. But when I couldn't find Guntram in the lodge, I checked the library, not wishing to find him there.

But he was. And given his uncombed beard and bloodshot eyes, he hadn't slept at all the night before. He had two leaning stacks of books on either side of him, and he looked committed to poring over each tome before giving up.

I left him alone. I tried to get my mind off things by offering to help Sipho out. The homestead takes a ridiculous amount of upkeep, and even though Sipho has an incredible work ethic, she can't get it all done by herself. During the course of the day, I harvested some kale (ugh) from the garden, mended a few crooked fenceposts, and even washed some of Sipho's tools. By midday, Sipho thanked me for my time and replaced my broken defensive charm, but then insisted I take a break. I didn't have the heart to tell her I wanted to stay busy. She'd only ask me to explain why.

On the way back to the lodge, I bumped into Azar heading out toward the woods. She had a pouch of food draped around her shoulder that indicated she didn't intend to come back for a while.

"Leaving already?" I asked.

"Why, yes," she replied. "Is that so surprising?"

"What about the fire watch? Aren't we supposed to patrol Siuslaw?"

"Did Guntram not tell you? That task is finished. We anticipate no further fire threat."

If that was true, why was Guntram pouring over texts in the library as if our lives depended on it? But instead, I asked, "Where are you going?"

"I'm called to Mt. Hood. I wish I could say more, but the matter is urgent, so I must regrettably bid you a hasty farewell."

Yet another mystery, I thought as the forest swallowed her up. Mt. Hood kept cropping up. On another day, I might have tried to grill the details out of her, but today, I just felt deflated.

Deflation morphed into an intense depression when I caught sight of Tabitha and Darby not far away. Tabitha threw feathers in the air one at a time, yelling at Darby to use air pith to keep them aloft. Although Tabitha barked in her usual militaristic fashion, Darby seemed to enjoy the challenge, a bright smile plastered on her sweaty face.

Tabitha slapped on a wry grin of her own and suddenly tossed a whole handful toward her eyas. When Darby deftly executed a rapid set of air sigils that sent them straight back at Tabitha, they both burst into peals of what could only be described as giggles.

What kind of bizarro timeline had I stumbled upon where the Sassy Squad acted like besties and Jichan wanted absolutely nothing to do with me?

I refused to mope around the homestead all day. I opted for a walk.

Fechin caught me right outside the homestead's border. He flew to a nearby Douglas fir and squawked at me, feathers ruffling around his neck.

I stuck my tongue out at him. "I'm not getting into any trouble. Follow me around if you like. I have nothing to hide."

The bird did a little hopping dance on the branch that I interpreted as, "Don't mind if I do."

I ignored my unwanted companion as I aimlessly meandered. I had no destination in particular, just the opportunity to move my body and soak in the natural pith of the forest. A breeze filled my air pith. Streams for water. I rubbed against boulders for earth. And once I'd collected a decent amount of all three, I combined them to form a spark of fire which I used to keep me warm under the shade of the old growth canopy.

I purposely let my mind go blank, not allowing myself thoughts of others. Certainly not Guntram or Vincent. I pushed Rafe from my mind as well.

I focused solely on myself, a child of Nasci. On the surface I didn't come across like the meditative type, but honestly, being a shepherd did suit my personality. It gave me a purpose in life, disconnected from the useless garbage we hang onto in modern society: social media profiles, busy jobs without much output, accumulating wealth. I'd never cared for those things. I just wanted to make a real difference. Leave an impact. And it would be nice to belong too, but I knew from experience not to get too fixated on that.

I focused my mind on the beauty of the wilderness around me. How each tree had started from a single small seed but now loomed above me. The imperfect path of a flittering butterfly. A hawk soaring past with prey in its talons. A music hummed, one that I could uniquely identify as a shepherd. A slithering of movement in taller brush. Tweets and chirps both near and far. Insects singing out for mates. It wasn't pith, exactly, but still Nasci's energy, one that relaxed me far more than any pill in a bottle could have. I don't know when exactly, but somewhere in the middle of this mindless trek my headache disappeared.

It would, of course, not last.

I surprised myself by somehow ending up at Carol and Dennis's highway rest stop. I didn't aim for this destination. The forest had simply taken me there. I must have walked many miles farther than I had anticipated.

I hesitated, lingering in the trees as I spied the

only customer vehicle in the parking lot slowly drive away. I didn't really wish to break the tranquil mood I'd managed to find. But already the spell had been broken. A sense of foreboding filled my body as all my worries came rushing back —Guntram's anger, Vincent's betrayal, and Rafe's proposal.

Well, if I was going to brood, I might as well do it with a pop.

Fechin cawed at me as my boots crunched gravel in the parking lot. "I'm going in for a drink." I rolled my eyes at his objection. "You want to tell Guntram that, you go right ahead." Then I pushed open the dirty glass door.

This time, Carol hunkered down near the cash register on a stool. She wore polyester pants, a wrinkled blouse, and a short curly hairstyle that put her in the age category of "above middle-age, probably."

"Hey, Ina," Carol called, not bothering to glance up from her dollar store puzzle book. How she could identify me with just her eyebrows, I'd never know. "Dennis said you wanted to buy batteries the other day. We still ain't got any."

"Oh, that's okay, I'm buying a pop today." I made my way to a back wall of carbonation-filled goodness and picked out my favorite brand. Hello, my diabetic friend. I took it halfway up to the counter before I belatedly realized I didn't have any cash. Groaning, I turned to put it back away.

Carol glanced up at my muttering. "Something

wrong?"

"I forgot my wallet. I can't buy this."

Carol surprised me by rummaging around behind the counter. "No problem. Someone else has you covered."

I halted in mid-stride. "What?"

"Just bring the darn thing up here and I'll explain."

I slowly shuffled up to the counter as she put a small brown paper bag and a twenty-dollar bill on the counter. She rang me up with the cash, handed me coins and bills as change, and said, "Some forest service guy was looking for you."

My mouth went dry. I swallowed to create some moisture. "Did he have a name?"

She scratched her head. "Gerrick? Gonzales?"

"Garcia?"

"That's it. Garcia." She motioned toward the bag. "He left this for you."

I warily peered inside. There was a prepaid white cell phone and charger with a handwritten note scribbled on the back of a receipt.

It read, "I'll explain everything. Call me." Signed V.G.

"You guys have a falling out or something?" Carol asked as I threw the empty bag and note away in a nearby garbage can.

"Or something," I answered on my way out.

"He seemed nice!" Carol offered before the door could shut behind me.

"I'm sure he did," I said as I stalked off into the

forest. "They always do."

CHAPTER 17

OF COURSE, VINCENT would leave me a package at Carol and Dennis's. He not only knew the approximate location of the homestead since he'd visited there once, I'd also mentioned the store to him during our various text message exchanges. And knowing how hard it was for me to get cash, he'd decided to leave some money to sweeten the deal.

I shouldn't have accepted the peace offering, but I'm weak-willed when it comes to carbonated beverages. Vincent also guessed I wouldn't be able to resist turning on the cell phone and checking the voicemail. As I stomped back through the forest, I listened to the recorded message I predicted would be there. I flinched as his familiar voice came out loud and clear over the phone.

"Ina, I know what you think you saw. Let me explain things to you but not in a message. Please call me."

I powered the phone back down. I didn't want to hear excuses. Vincent would figure out one way or another that I'd been given the phone, but even knowing the homestead's location, he couldn't really find me. Only followers of Nasci could see past the magical façade Sipho had created, making the entire property appear like another mountain in the Cascades. I could only imagine how frustrating that must have been for Vincent, locked outside a mountain with absolutely no way in.

"Serves him right." I shoved the phone in my hoodie pouch. My fingers smashed against something hard and I cursed.

I withdrew the offending object, the cracked stone. I'd forgotten all about the weird object Rafe had given me at the hospital. Too many other things had taken up my headspace. I studied it for a second but had no idea what I was supposed to do with a rock.

"What's with guys giving me useless junk lately?" I bent my arm to fling the stone out into the woods. I needed an outlet to get rid of all this sentimental crud.

Fechin's screeching interrupted me. He swooped down and gave me a bird lecture.

"Yeah, I got it. I'm going back to Sipho's." I returned the stone back to my pocket, heading out toward the nearest wisp channel. I supposed I should try to patch things up with Guntram.

But once back at the homestead, I found my augur fast asleep. Not in the lodge like a sane person, but in the library, his arms draped over a table and head resting on a yellowed book. He snored loudly, a little string of spit falling from the corner of his mouth and pooling on the wood.

My heart hurt for him. Whatever was happening out there with the weird not-vaetturs and messed-up breaches was obviously tearing him apart, but I didn't understand why. He and I had been training together for weeks before this all went down, so he couldn't have directly caused any of it. And he'd refused to tell me what he knew. I could only readjust his askew cloak around his shoulders so he wouldn't waste extra fire pith to keep warm while he slept.

The rest of the homestead also lay quiet as the sun went down, most of the occupants diurnal. The only active creature I ran into as the full moon rose was Kam, Sipho's chocolate-colored mountain lion. She trotted across a field to shove her forehead into my palm, demanding affection as she purred. I was more than happy to oblige.

"What should I do, Kam?" I asked her. "Call Vincent back or not?"

Kam cajoled me into giving her a thorough belly rub and then plopped onto the grass, tucking her legs underneath her chest. A wide yawn exposed her sharp teeth, and she buried her face in her paws.

"You're right," I said, straightening. "I probably should sleep on it too."

And despite a bit of tossing and turning in my lodge bedroom, I did eventually manage to do just that.

* * *

I found myself in the middle of a roaring blaze.

Choking, I stumbled through the burning forest, no idea how to get out. I tried to create a continuous cycle of fire pith, absorbing and releasing it in a continuous flow, but the flames quickly overwhelmed me. I couldn't get my fire aura started, and without it, I would succumb to the heat.

A spine-tingling cry cut through the dull roar around me. Out of the flames, the fire demon formed, all limbs and hollow eyes. I figured I would die even as I raised my arms to protect my head from its stubby attack.

Then it struck me and I fell, fell, fell...

...onto the dirt floor of the lodge.

I woke from my nightmare with a whimper, stray straw stuck to my cheeks. My entire body lay drenched in a thin layer of sweat, and my hoodie had managed to twist itself in an almost stranglehold. I had to tug and pull at the drawstrings to reposition it correctly on my torso.

"Stupid dream," I grumbled to myself on the final yank.

Something hard slid from the kangaroo pouch and thudded on the floor. Rafe's cracked stone. I grabbed it instinctively, not thinking much of it until my damp hands touched the surface.

A flash of blue light suddenly lit the fissures of its surface.

"Ah!" I yelped as I jerked away from it.

The blue light faded as it hit the ground, and the stone returned to normal.

I took a second to gather my bearings. Moonlight streaked in through the room's glassless window. An owl hooted somewhere deep in the forest. Everything appeared very normal, and the rock sat there pretty as you please, not glowing. Wiping my sweaty palms dry on my shorts, I poked it a couple more times.

Still no more glowing lights.

I almost dismissed the whole ordeal as an aftereffect of my dream. I don't normally have them, but when I do, they were always full of messed up crap. But I'd never hallucinated before. And that soft blue light reminded me of something I'd seen before. I just couldn't remember what.

Besides, I was awake now. My stomach gurgled. The lodge had only slim, healthy pickings, but a few dried fruit slices would be better than trying to fall back asleep on adrenaline and an empty stomach. I grabbed the stone and trudged out into the hallway.

Light from the ever-glowing fireplace danced on the walls and ceiling as I made my way into the open common area. Deep shadows formed around the kitchen, the chairs, and especially the shallow pool, which sent refractions of beams every which way as muted firelight hit its surface.

I froze. I remembered now where I'd seen a weird blue glow from inside a rock. A kembar stone.

Several weeks ago, when we'd fought the mishipeshu, we discovered that it'd traveled quickly between distant bodies of water using linked kembar stones. The stones acted a lot like wisp channels, except you needed to cast advanced water sigils to activate it. After defeating the mishipeshu, the shepherds had debated how the panther had created such sophisticated magical objects, since vaetturs are generally creatures of blunt force. The only two theories we came up with were either the panther had indeed made the stones itself, or perhaps the stones had been left by a shepherd so long ago that they had been forgotten.

I found the latter explanation unlikely. Shepherds were notorious for passing down knowledge. With a penchant for archiving even some of the most useless information, I wondered how something as important as kembar stones between lakes in the Talol Wilds had been lost over time.

And now I potentially held a kembar stone in my hand. But how to tell for sure?

I shuffled to the edge of the pool. All the other stones we'd ever found had laid at the bottom of a lake. I tossed Rafe's stone in.

Once submerged, it pulsated with that soft blue glow again, an imitation will o' the wisp. I inhaled sharply as I realized the sweat on my hands must have activated it back in my bedroom.

I waded barefoot in after it. I kneeled down,

making sure not to get my butt drenched as I crouched over the stone. If this thing behaved like the others before, then executing an underwater breathing sigil should take me to the other kembar stone that connected with this one.

I hesitated. I'd never felt threatened by Rafe. He could have hurt me any number of ways as I snoozed unconscious at the hospital. But he had been content to keep me company until I awoke. Still, it was a whole other leap of faith to teleport myself to wherever he wanted me to go. In the middle of the night no less.

But then, what else could I do? I couldn't just ignore this stone, and given how little Guntram trusted me, I couldn't tell him about it without risking further wrath.

So, I did what I do best. I forged ahead. I plunged forward in the water so that my entire front side submerged into the pool. I let my mind go blank and executed a perfect underwater breathing sigil, complete with continuous pith flow. The kembar stone reacted by spinning me around in its strange undertow, much deeper than the lodge pool itself, and within seconds, it transported me far away from Sipho's homestead to the stone's sister site.

CHAPTER 18

I'D TRAVELED THROUGH a kembar stone once, and it had led me from the depths of one lake into another. I expected to find myself disoriented in a large body of water needing to find my way to the surface.

Instead, I wound up cramped inside a half-filled bathtub.

Caught completely off-guard, I attempted to stand, but my bare feet slid on the slick white porcelain. I managed to grab a handful of plastic curtain, only to have that come crashing down on my head as I yanked too hard and dislodged the shower rod. I fell in a heap, entangled in several sheets as I splashed in six inches of water. Kicking and yelling, I didn't even realize someone was trying to help me until the entire bundle flew away from me, exposing my night-accustomed sight to an intense white light.

A disembodied voice broke through the glow. "Ina, calm down. It's me."

I squinted, shapes slowly coming into view. A dark shadow formed into pretty boy Rafe wearing a long-sleeved T-shirt and jogging pants. He offered a hand to help me stand. I noticed a nondescript toilet and sink behind him as he heaved me out of the tub. He supported me as he led me, dripping onto the hard carpet of a small bedroom. A queen bed adorned with an ugly blue and pink floral comforter dominated most of the room. Beside it, a microwave lounged atop a dorm style fridge. Opposite the bed, a square stand held a TV. A worn table rounded out the bland ensemble.

"Where are we?" I asked as he escorted me to the table's upholstered chair. He didn't seem to mind that I dripped a trail of bath water behind me.

"My motel room in Florence. I'm glad you decided to come."

I leaped back to my feet and threw open the outside door of the room. A parking lot, half-filled with vehicles, stretched on toward a road, flanked on all sides by long brown buildings with evenly spaced doors. The far end of one building had a sign saying it housed an office and an indoor pool. On the road, a sedan's headlights whizzed past, and I could make out two lanes going in either direction, with a turning lane in between. It must have been Highway 101.

"Believe me now?" Rafe asked.

I twirled around and said louder than I intended. "You connected the kembar stone to here?"

A loud thudding on the wall interrupted our conversation. "Shuddup, you two!" a man's voice growled. "I'm tryin' to sleep!"

I cringed in embarrassment, but Rafe scowled. "What a jerk. Come, Ina." He grabbed a flat map from the table, shooed me outside, and locked the motel door. "Let's go for a walk."

I assumed Rafe would take us out to the sidewalk that lined the highway, but he surprised me by walking behind the most remote building of the motel complex. A decent-sized wooded area lay behind it, not quite as invigorating as an old growth forest but wild just the same. I would have enjoyed it a lot more with my hiking boots, though. Every so often I'd step on a pointy twig with my bare sole and wince.

Once we'd receded far enough into the trees, Rafe took a deep breath. "Doesn't that feel better?"

It did. The air pith felt purer back here, the trees a natural filter. But despite the full moon, little light made its way down to the ground.

"Dark though," I said.

Rafe raised his free hand, and before I could guess his intent, he drew a cross with a vertical line. A little flame shot from his fingertip, glowing for a few seconds before petering out completely.

"I wish I had a better light," he said.

I gasped. "You can draw fire sigils!" I lit my own fingertips for a sustained flame.

A hint of sadness lingered on Rafe's lips. "I can only perform a few basic sigils, and even then, only for a very short time and with the aid of this." He pulled back his sleeve to show a chain metal bracelet strapped above his elbow. Four thin slats of metal hung at intervals, each with a carved symbol that stood for a different element.

"Are those charms?" I asked incredulously.

Rafe nodded. "I can't hold pith in my body like you can. When I harvest it from vaetturs, I have to store it in these."

My mind reeled with a thousand questions. "Where did you learn so much about shepherds? And how did you make the charms and kembar stones? Those aren't 'basic' by any stretch. They require complex mastery above even me."

Rafe folded his arms and studied me carefully. "You can find knowledge if you look for it. There are others like me who've figured out how to craft items such as these." He pointed to both his charms and the stones. "I've used the kembar stones in recent months to make travel in the area more convenient for me. They're laid out all over the state, although some have recently gone missing."

I held back a gasp. The missing stones had likely been due to Guntram, who had destroyed the mishipeshu's kembar routes that we knew about. I had known deep down that someone else besides the mishipeshu or long-ago shepherds had created those things. It made so much more sense.

Still, the thought that others out there could manipulate the elements like shepherds put me on edge. "If you can do all that, what do you want with me? Why bring me here?"

"Because we have a common enemy." Rafe unfolded the map he'd grabbed from the room. Inside contained the topography of Oregon. He spread it out under my fingerflame so I could see where he'd written on it in permanent marker. I recognized all the places he'd marked on the map.

"You've been following the fire demon too," I said, pointing to the logging operation where we'd taken it down.

"Fire demon?" Rafe asked confused.

"You know, the big ugly fire shadowy thing? No hands and feet? Creepy eyes?"

"Ah," Rafe said, understanding lighting his face. "You call it a demon. I call it a golem. And yes, I've been monitoring the golem too. It's connected to the bull vaettur after all."

"How so?"

Rafe raised an eyebrow. "Shouldn't you know this already? Haven't the other shepherds told you anything about it?"

I sighed. "No. They said an eyas like me doesn't need to know."

Rafe threw me a sympathetic smile. "I thought as much. Shepherds do love pulling rank. Let me fill you in then. This," he indicated the trail where I'd met him, "is where our trouble started. I assume since you were in the proximity, you found the odd breach?"

"Yes." I shivered, remembering the awful buzzing sensation. "It didn't feel like an ordinary rip between dimensions. Something about it was different."

"That's because humans caused it."

My breathing froze for a moment. "What? How is that even possible?"

Rafe narrowed his eyes. "It's possible because humankind does not care for Nasci at all. Surely you've noticed how someone had already violated that patch of earth?"

I remembered the trashed, illegal campsite. "Yeah, it was pretty bad."

"Destroying Nasci's natural world isn't just a direct attack on her. It's also a weakening between her world and Letum's. Imagine removing the barbed wire from atop a fence. With one layer of defense gone, you can scale the fence, and voila! You're inside."

"But vaetturs generally appear in the woods, as far away from people as possible. I've never even heard of a vaettur attacking anywhere near a town until the demon, I mean golem, in Mapleton."

"Normal vaetturs don't," Rafe agreed. "They hunt animals and dryants for pith. But the stuff coming out of these breaches—" he flicked his fingers on the various attack points on the map, "— they don't act like normal vaetturs. They're more vulnerable to Nasci's power. They don't have the skills to create breaches themselves. They can only cross where vile humans have interfered. And in a twist of irony, they must also prey on the weakest of Nasci's creatures." He paused to pierce me with his gaze. "They stalk humans."

I ignored his talk of human vileness. I was used

to hearing that kind of talk from other shepherds. I focused instead on his more shocking statement.

"You think they'll actually hurt people?"

"Consider what happened, Ina. The golem appeared right outside Mapleton before you scared it off."

I pointed at another spot on Rafe's map circled in black, connecting the dots with him. "And then it tried to take down a clearcut logging operation full of workers."

Rafe nodded. "It was targeting people."

"There's still something I don't understand. We banished the bull, but we couldn't do that to the golem. We had to…" I searched for the right words. "…siphon off its fiery magic. Make it dissipate."

Rafe had an answer for everything. "That's because a golem is a special kind of creature. A being of pure pith. Golems must be ripped apart by their very essence."

I bit my lip, filtering all this new information in my head. This went against a lot of what Guntram had always taught me about Letum and the vaetturs that invaded our world. And yet, it also connected the pieces of the broken puzzle I'd been unable to understand.

"Well, the weirdo breach is sealed, the bull's banished, and the golem taken care of. We're in the clear, right?"

Rafe gave me the chills by shaking his head. "There's another golem on the loose."

"What?" I cried. "How can you know that?"

Rafe's calm demeanor cracked, anger marring his face. "Because I'm not a nobody!" he shouted. He then took a step back, composing himself. "Sorry. I get carried away. Shepherds believe they understand everything, but in truth, they comprehend very little. And their actions may very well doom all of us."

Unsure how to react to his shifting moods, I asked, "What do you mean?"

"Shepherds focus mostly on what's happening in the natural world. They want to believe in a strict order, but life is too complex for such simplistic categories. There are people out there, like me—" he flashed fire at his fingertip once more, "—who don't fit so neatly into one of their boxes. But we have value too. We deserve a chance to protect Nasci in our own ways."

I sympathized with Rafe. I may be a shepherd, but I came into it via untraditional methods, much older than other eyases. As Tabitha loved to point out, I was a "haggard" who began training as an adult. If Guntram hadn't believed in me despite this supposed flaw, I'd probably be living some meaningless life, still seeing dryants occasionally on a hike, wondering if I was going crazy.

I grabbed the back of his hand holding the map. "I get how you feel."

Rafe gazed deeply at me. He put a second hand on top of mine, so that my fingers became sandwiched in between his. "Thank you."

Blushing, I withdrew my hand. "What do you

know about the other golem?"

Rafe reopened the map. "I encountered it at the logging operation. It got away before the other shepherds noticed, but it roams the area yet. Given the trajectory of its recent activity, I think it's heading west."

"West?" My eyes drew a line from the bull attack to Mapleton to the logging site. "There isn't much left west to go, but..." I trailed off in horror.

"Yes." Rafe nodded. "Florence."

Like most coastal towns, Florence butted up against a major forest. My blood ran cold at the image of that fiery monster torching up a place where nine thousand people called home.

"Are you sure?" I asked.

"It's been my experience that these things are drawn to the largest concentration of people. They found Mapleton first, the nearest town to the breach, then moved onto the clearcutters. There's really nowhere else to go." He smoothed out the map once again. "Except Florence."

"You think we should stake out Florence?" I asked, frowning.

"No, I think you should."

"You mean shepherds?" The thought of asking the others to help me monitor people produced a dry laugh. "The other shepherds don't care what happens to normal towns."

"Then you'll have to do it alone."

I scooted away from Rafe. "Look, I love the confidence, but you've got the wrong shepherd. I saw how much sigil work it took three shepherds of higher rank than me to take down the first golem. I don't have those kinds of fire skills, and my lightning does nothing to these things."

"You don't need any of that," Rafe said. "You should simply absorb the golem's pith."

"Yeah, about that. I tried that with the last golem." I shivered, remembering how awful it had made me feel afterward. "Not a good idea. That stuff messes with you."

"Vaettur pith is a kind of poison, but you're strong enough to withstand it with the right tools." Rafe removed the bracelet from his elbow. "Here, take this."

I backed up a step. "Why?"

"It will allow you to store Letum's energy in a purer form, taking the edge off a little."

I refused to touch the bracelet. "No, I can't."

"I can't do the things you do, Ina. My magical capabilities are very weak. I can only absorb so much vaettur pith." He pointed straight at my heart. "But you're near legendary. A shepherd that can master lightning. You could absorb the entire fire golem and lock its power within this charm, no problem."

"But that's yours."

"Then borrow it. You can always give it back to me when you're done."

I couldn't see any harm in taking the charm. I didn't have to use it unless I wanted to. Still, I hesitated. "I don't know."

"You are the only one who can do this task," Rafe insisted. "By your own admission, the other shepherds won't come. I've tried and failed. Normal people can't even see these things. Either you do it, or the fire golem has free reign over Florence."

He had a point. I couldn't offer any other option either.

"Okay." I took the bracelet from him. It weighed heavier than the charms around my neck, more clunky. I adjusted it around my own arm.

Rafe walked me back to the motel. He told me he would be here when I'd finished attacking the golem.

"Won't you come with me?" I asked.

But Rafe shook his head. "I'm vulnerable without my charms. I would be as useful to you as a can of gasoline fighting against fire."

"Then I'd better go back and get prepared." No way would I go vaettur hunting without boots. I headed for the bathroom, stepping back into the tub. The kembar stone glowed between my toes. "Wish me luck."

He touched my arm. "One last thing. Promise you won't tell the others about me." A melancholy expression crossed his face. "I doubt the other shepherds would want someone like me interfering in what they consider their own sacred duty."

I had no intention of telling anyone about Rafe. "Okay. I won't. I promise."

Rafe gave me a soft smile, then leaned over to whisper. "Good luck, Ina. I have faith in you."

I didn't reply, laying down as best as I could in the cramped tub. I drew the underwater breathing sigil and ducked my face into the water. My head spun as I clenched the kembar stone in my fist. I should have been concentrating on the possible fight ahead and how I would possibly be able to take down a fire golem by myself, but instead all I could hear was Rafe's whisper in my ear.

Someone who believed in me for a change.

CHAPTER 19

THE STONE PLOPPED me as a wet mess in the middle of the lodge pool, but anticipation flowed in my veins despite the indignity. I hid the kembar stone in the driest place I could think of, a high cupboard in the kitchen. I had to stand on the stone countertop to shove it back as far as possible, but once there, I felt confident no one would find it. You couldn't even see it at ground level. Satisfied, I grabbed some dried fruit, laced on my hiking boots, and skipped outside, hoping to escape the property as quietly as possible.

The homestead remained fast asleep in the pitch darkness, save for a flickering light in the library. A shadow passed by the open doorway. I could make out Guntram rummaging around inside. He'd apparently gotten up and went right back to work on his project.

A teeny part of me wanted to run and tell him everything—how I knew all about what the golems were and I had a plan to stop another one. But Guntram had made it crystal clear that I'd been in the wrong to save the geezer in Mapleton. He'd never understand, and I wouldn't let him discourage me from saving other people too.

"I'm doing the right thing, Guntram," I whispered to his silhouette. "Even if you don't think so."

Veering toward the south, a flurry of movement caught my attention. A score of ravens roosted on the library roof, mostly around the eaves with their beaks tucked into their heads. One young bird, however, had clearly been tasked with keeping watch toward the lodge, probably for me. Head listing as he nodded off, he nevertheless saw me and gave a brief squawk, flapping his wings in my direction.

"Shh!" I hissed. The dozing birds stirred, but none awoke. If I didn't quiet this young upstart soon, he'd alert the others and I'd never be able to leave the homestead. Desperate, I patted my kangaroo pouch, but the phone wouldn't help me at all.

But I did feel something hard and round in my shorts side pocket. Pulling it out, I found a quarter Carol had given me in change.

The raven's thrashing quietened. He cocked his head at the coin.

I grinned, dangling it. "You like shiny stuff, don't you?"

He hopped around, clearly excited about the quarter.

"Okay then," I slid the coin into my fist, gathering air pith in my arm. "Go get it!"

I threw the quarter as far as I could in the opposite direction of where I wanted to go, drawing a sideways S to give it some extra distance. Its dual surfaces gleamed in the moonlight, a bright beacon. The raven glided furiously after it.

I sprinted toward the tree line, making it into the shadows in record time. I seriously doubted such a juvenile plan would actually work, but the raven never followed, and I plunged into the wisp channel without any snitch on my heels.

* * *

When you're pumped for a fight, you want that fight to happen right away. It kinda kills the buzz when you're hurrying around just to wait for something to happen. And yet, there I was, standing on a ridge above Florence, which spread out past the trees below me on the flat plains that drifted toward the Siuslaw River.

I had no idea when or where the fire golem might arrive, so I paced about like a tiger in a cage, checking for smoke far to the north and then looping back around to the south, then back again. Rafe's bracelet dug into my skin underneath the hoodie, a constant reminder of the looming threat. But as the sun rose high above me and nothing happened, the weight became less of a warning and more of an irritation.

Too much empty time leaves your mind to wander. I asked myself a billion times how Rafe could be so sure about this fire golem, or if I should even trust him. When I finally convinced myself I'd committed to finishing this, that led to thoughts of my argument with Guntram and how I'd let him down. Once I ditched that guilt, Vincent and our current impasse in communication dominated my thoughts.

On a whim, I powered up the phone again. Vincent hadn't called again, but he had sent a huge text that the phone carrier broke up into many disjointed chunks.

"Wall of text crits me for fatal damage," I grumbled. I vowed not to read it, but curiosity and boredom broke that promise pretty quickly.

"Ina," it read. "I wish I could explain this to you in a conversation and not in a text, but you're not giving me a lot of options here. You must be upset seeing Christy and me together. She's my ex-wife."

I almost dropped the phone at that revelation. Ex-wife? Vincent was in his 20s. I tried to imagine marrying so young before I read on.

"We were high school sweethearts. Really young and in love, but it didn't last once we grew up a little. It ended pretty badly. Tore our families apart. They were close and encouraged the relationship. But time heals some wounds, and we've become friends the past few years."

"Friends," I snorted to myself, remembering how she stroked Vincent's face in the car. "Friends with benefits."

"But not friends with benefits," Vincent's text went on, as if reading my thoughts. "Just normal friends. At least that's what I want. Christy wants more but has respected my choice not to get back together."

"Until you started fondling in the car," I grumbled.

"I don't know how much you saw. It probably looked like a date. It really wasn't. I was in town for a business meeting. We met on a whim for dinner, I gave her a ride home, and I drove back to Florence."

"So, you're saying I just stumbled upon your purely platonic not-date with an ex?" I asked the phone.

"I'm not going to lie to you. I do sometimes stay the night at her house—to visit friends, go to football games, that kind of thing. But we haven't been intimate since we divorced. I swear to God."

At this confession, I wanted to chuck the phone down a nearby ledge. Was he building plausible deniability into his so-called explanation? How stupid did he think I was?

"I never meant to hurt your feelings," he continued. "I'm not even sure where you and I stand. But I wanted you to understand I am truly not attached to anyone else. I'm single, and I didn't lead you on in the apartment."

"Too late," I told the phone, ignoring the sting in my eyes. "I don't care about your relationship status. I know mine, and it's currently set to 'go away.'"

"Please call me when you get this."

I shoved the phone so hard into my pocket, I jammed a finger. "Not a chance," I said. "Not now, not ever." Determined not to dwell on the message, I glanced back at the horizon.

And that's when I spotted the plume of smoke to the south.

Florence, for all its coastal glamor, is a rural town. It was possible someone had lit a small fire in their backyard for some innocuous reason. I ran down the ridge to check it out. Beyond the tree line, I zipped across the short shores Ackerley Lake, then busted up a second incline that overlooked Munsel Lake.

The smoke curled up above a long neighborhood of houses. And it was growing. Definitely a real fire.

I removed my boots, holding them in one hand as I stepped into the water. Tapping into my water pith, I drew a triangle over waves and sprinted across the top of Munsel. The relatively still surface of the lake flexed like sponge beneath my feet, forcing me to lean one way or the other to maintain my balance.

I found a landing dock not far away and raced for it. There was one older guy there with a sleeveless jacket and jeans. He'd backed up his pick-up truck to the water and had a motorboat halfway in the water, ready to go for a spin on the lake. Fortunately, he had his back to me as he messed around with his hitch, so he never saw me running at him from across the lake. That would have been awkward. Instead, I dashed across the parking lot unnoticed and out onto the highway that fed into it.

Panting from exertion, I took a second to realign my position. Down here at low elevation, I couldn't see much due to the tall trees on either side of the road. Hoping for a better vantage point, I planted my feet wide in a sigil stance, then focused my air pith. I drew a short series of spiral Ss and, with a grimace, released an air blast underneath my feet.

Guntram may glide around with no problem, but I had major control issues. I would have loved to fly up several hundred feet to examine the fire, but I had to make do with twenty. Even then, I wobbled like a preschooler without training wheels. The view didn't provide me much other than a direction. Even at this distance, flames licked toward the sky, snaking toward the houses.

The golem definitely meant to burn some people.

I let go of my air pith so I could fall back down, drawing an occasional spiral S to ease the descent. My graceless butt landed on the highway with an undignified smack anyway.

"Ouch," I groaned. It smarted but no broken bones at least. I laced my boots back on. As I stood, a flash of silver loomed down the highway. Someone was driving my way. I didn't have time to explain what I was doing in the middle of the road. I had to face this thing.

I dashed into the trees at the same time as the

car screeched to a halt, not far from where I'd just been. I thought I heard a car door slam, but I didn't look behind me as I evaded thorns and bramble. No sane person would run after me into these thick woods. With any luck, they'd notice the fire and call emergency services to help contain the blaze.

The air temperature rose fifteen degrees, a sign I neared my target. I passed a handful of animals scurrying away from the heat. At least the few animals that lived this close to town could handle themselves. I didn't have to evacuate them.

It was the people in those houses I worried about.

I summoned a pocket of air before entering an ashen wasteland, most of the tree trunks sizzling red with fire. I knew I was in over my head. I'd never entered the heart of a forest fire without other shepherds before, and my fire skills couldn't begin to contain this. But I was too close to civilization. No shepherd would come to help me.

I was truly on my own.

I steeled myself as I approached the heat center. Burnt debris crackled around me, my air pocket protesting. When a spurt of smoke blew near my face, I switched to absorbing fire pith. All the other energy stores in my pithways faded as I became a fire absorption machine, every corner of my body filling with fire. I tried to smooth out the proper rhythm of intake and release, to let the fire pith leave and enter me in a continuous flow, or I would never stand a chance against the golem. I even managed to convince myself I just needed a few minutes, and I'd master a fire skill that had eluded me since I became a shepherd.

And that's when a fire stream shot out of the black fog and hit me square in the stomach.

The sucker punch sent me backward, right into a massive tree trunk that had refused to yield to the inferno around it. I saw stars as my head whipped backward, cracking against a knot in the wood.

As I slid down to my knees, the fire golem appeared, as tall as a basketball hoop, an angry silhouette against its self-made purgatory. It roared, the sound sending sharp pinpricks up and down my spine. I wobbled with dizziness as it charged across the clearing toward me, flinging a fireball from the tip of its stump arm.

A shimmering shield appeared in front of me seconds before the fireball would have melted my face. My defensive charm had kicked in. It took the edge off the impact but sent shivers of sweltering force back at me, like a heavy slap to my face. Having activated, the pith inside the defensive charm weakened.

I might not survive a second attack.

That realization spurred me into action. I grabbed onto my water charm, letting its soothing chill speed through my pithways. I drew a series of Vs with lines jutting out the top, creating a water stream to throw back at the golem.

The golem's hollow eyes widened in pain as the

water ripped the arm holding a second fireball right off its shoulder socket. The enflamed woods trembled with its shrieks as it stumbled.

I had to finish this now, before I turned to ash like everything else around me. I grabbed onto Rafe's bracelet, the fire charm between one thumb and forefinger.

The fire golem recovered from my water attack, its shortened arm growing back to its full length. As it expanded, the golem let out sparks of fire from the top of its head, both elbows, even its torso. They curved and curled together like a braided ribbon, hoping to melt me like a little wax candle on the spot.

I jerked to the side, thinking to avoid the assault, but realized sooner or later I would have to absorb this thing. Wincing, I braced myself for the fire golem's energy, opening up my pithways.

Even knowing how awful absorbing its vaettur fire would feel didn't lessen the impact. Stabbing sensations wracked me as it ravaged my pithways. My head pounded in agony as fire overwhelmed all my senses. If I hadn't already been holding onto the bracelet, I probably would have fainted right then and there, a death sentence in a solo confrontation.

I couldn't just keep absorbing. I concentrated on Rafe's fire charm in between my fingers.

"Please," I begged. "Let this work."

Then I pushed the vaettur's fire pith into it.

I didn't realize it was possible, but the pain intensified. Rafe's charm did absorb the golem's pith, but it felt like a crayon getting threaded through a needle, and unfortunately my body was the needle in this analogy. My pithways threatened to explode from the strain.

A roar rang in my ears. I thought at first it might be my own voice but through slit eyelids, I caught sight of a wildly oscillating blaze. The terrified golem had attempted to run away, but I pulled it back. It raised its arms to ignite more fires, but I absorbed that energy too. As it flailed, trying to do anything to stop me, its giant form shrunk a few feet.

I couldn't break contact. If I did, the golem would get away. I was the only thing standing between it and innocent people. That righteous fury gave me the resolve to hold my ground, breathing through anguish to get the job done.

What felt like an eternity probably only lasted a few minutes. I forced every last ounce of fire pith I could into Rafe's charm, and as I did, the fire golem shriveled like an elderly man growing in reverse. Soon my height, then smaller, until finally it couldn't have stood taller than a golden retriever. The golem seemed almost cute at the end, the size of a baby kitten and mewing pitifully, but I knew it was one stroke away from raging back to full form. With a final push, I absorbed the rest of its energy into my pithways.

It vanished in a pop, and with it gone, the forest fire lost some of its edge. The fire raged on, but with the source extinguished, it no longer consumed everything in its path. Instead it simmered with no real intention behind it, an orchestra without a conductor.

Which was a good thing, too, because I fell into a quagmire of soot and blacked out from exertion.

CHAPTER 20

"INA!"

Through the endless haze, someone called my name. I couldn't see anything at first. Couldn't move. My core felt stiff as a board, enmeshed into whatever muck I had fallen into.

"Ina!"

Someone shoved me over, and a bright orange glow lit up behind my eyelids. Groaning, I blinked to assuage its effects.

Vincent's concerned face slowly came into focus. His hands poked around my arms and back. "Can you stand?" he asked frantically.

Sensations returned to me in a flood. A terrible headache. Lingering spasms in all my muscles. But the anger came from confronting this divorced two-timer. I latched onto that.

"What are you doing here?" I demanded.

He had the audacity to scowl at me. "Saving your mopey ass. Unless nature wizards often take naps in the middle of forest fires."

His words brought the environment back into focus. I was still in the same spot where I'd drained the fire golem. The trees continued to burn around us, leaving only a thin thirty-degree window of perimeter that had not yet caught fire. Our only escape.

Vincent pointed toward that sanctuary. "We gotta go. Now."

He wrapped his arms underneath my shoulders and dragged my torso upwards. I struggled to stand, not in control of my joints after the attack. Bits of staticky pinpricks emanated from Rafe's bracelet, but I ignored that to focus on taking a few timid steps.

"Can you walk?" Vincent asked.

"I'll make it," I snapped.

Vincent did not let go, one arm tight around my waist as I lumbered forward. I leaned against him for added support, both loving and hating how much I enjoyed feeling his body close to mine, even in this dire situation.

"How the hell did you find me?" I asked as we inched our way forward.

"We'll talk about it later."

"We'll talk about it now."

"Are you serious?" he cried.

I dug in my heels, refusing to budge. "What do you think?"

His face reddened, this time not from the heat. "I put an app on your phone that allows me to track it whenever it's powered on."

"What?" I screamed.

"I just wanted to talk to you, okay?" he yelled

right back. "I knew you were upset, but you wouldn't let me explain myself. The app notified me that you were nearby, so I drove in this direction. I saw you diving into the forest and followed you."

The silver car! I felt so stupid only now connecting the dots. "You ran after me into a forest fire?"

"I'm not an idiot," he said in a tone that indicated that I was one. "I called 911 first. The fire department's already got fighters out near a residential street, but they don't have a lot of extra hands this far up." He tugged at my arm. "So, let's keep moving before we get stuck here."

He was not wrong. Our little window of safety had shrunk during our conversation, leaving only the thinnest slice left unmarred by fire. We hobbled together toward it as quickly as I could muster.

It wasn't fast enough. The two sides of the fire surged toward each other in a sudden wind gust. I grabbed onto my air charm to try to reverse the wind's course, but it was too late. The fires converged like hands clapping shut, blocking our exit before we could reach it.

"We're trapped!" Vincent cried, falling back as smoke billowed toward us.

Choking, I clutched him tighter, creating a barrier of air around us with the last of my air pith. It allowed us both to breathe. Then, much as it hurt, I began the cycle of absorbing and releasing fire pith again, redirecting what I could away from us. But even as I struggled to find a back-and-forth flow for all the fire around us, I knew this strategy was only temporary.

We'd burn up in a matter of minutes.

My own death made me sad, but rage consumed me thinking I'd go down with Vincent.

"Why?" I yelled at him. "Why'd you come out here to die?"

Vincent's fury matched my own. "Because I care about you, Ina!" Then he covered his face with his elbow as our air pocket waned.

As we both hunched over in coughing fits, my fury changed into despair. I didn't want to die out here, not surrounded by one of the very elements I should be able to control as a competent shepherd.

It couldn't end like this.

I spread my fingers out to the fire surrounding us. I wanted to redirect the swatch blocking our path, to allow us to pass through, but it was no use. Fire traced every corner of my pithways, on the verge of burning me from the inside out. No matter how much fire pith I released, more came sizzling to replace it. Smoke steamed off my skin.

"Dammit!" I screamed in frustration.

Beside me, Vincent's fingernails dug into my shoulder. "Calm down," he managed between hacks.

Calm.

Azar's words about fire rang through my head. *Fire allows for few emotions.*

I had to stay calm, focus my fire pith in a gentle

cycle, or it would consume me. But how? I lived my life by embracing my darker emotions, using them as fuel to push me forward. All my muscles clenched in rage as I struggled with how to let go.

Then Vincent slumped over, weakened by the smoke. His face slumped against mine, his lips accidentally brushing my brow.

Peace.

No matter how upset I'd been with Vincent these past few days, I never forgot sitting on his futon, his hair tousled from a recent shower. We had inched toward each other, inevitable as a force of nature. At that moment, I wanted nothing more than to be soaked up by his warmth, his spirit, his life.

And as he clung to me now, his consciousness fading, it suddenly didn't matter that he had an ex with benefits. It didn't matter if he'd lied to me. All that mattered was that one moment we'd almost shared together, how it had felt just right, like the world had finally aligned the way it was always meant to.

For a split second, it gave me peace.

And that's all the calm I needed. Fire pith flowed into my body, then out again, my pithways a giant cleansing fan. A white-hot glow illuminated my skin, the kind I'd seen on other shepherds as they deftly stood in the flames.

I could take the heat.

As gently as a mother lifting her newborn child into her arms, I embraced the flames crackling around me. I soaked them up my fingertips, through one arm, into my heart, and down the opposite limb, behind us. Sparks of fire redirected themselves out of our path of freedom, bursting behind us, in the past.

I'd created a way out.

I continued to redirect fire as I aided Vincent forward. He stumbled beside me, clinging onto me for dear life. He kept his head buried somewhere underneath my chin, so I had no idea if he knew we were escaping or not. I didn't care. It only mattered that I had everything under control.

That I could keep him safe.

We waded out into unburned territory. I no longer needed to redirect the fire as we walked outside of the immediate danger zone, but I continued to escort Vincent. He stopped coughing, his breath becoming more even, but his footing remained sluggish, his mind not 100% comprehending that we'd made it through.

We'd just broken through the trees into view of the highway when he collapsed to the ground, too weak from smoke inhalation to go farther. Not far down the road, his silver car was parked askance on the shoulder, the driver's side door still ajar. He'd rushed out so quickly, he'd forgotten to shut it.

"Ina," he gasped as I lowered his head gently down.

The unmistakable sound of sirens penetrated the air. Red flashing lights spun toward us from down the road. From where he lay prone, Vincent would be found immediately.

But I couldn't be seen.

"Everything's okay now," I whispered to him.

He tried to cinch onto my hoodie sleeve with his free hand. "Ina," he pleaded again.

But I didn't have time to talk. I pulled away from him, fleeing across the road and into the woods, out of sight.

I stuck around to watch the ambulance screech to a halt after noticing an injured man on the side of the road. An EMT hopped out to inspect Vincent, who had already gotten himself into a sitting position and was attempting to stand. When Vincent lurched vaguely toward me, I flinched with regret. He apparently hoped to catch up to me. But the EMT insisted he go toward the back of the ambulance instead.

I don't know how I managed with almost no water pith, but tears stung the corners of my eyes. I dabbed them away as I fled, trying desperately to hold onto that sense of peace that allowed me to control fire.

EPILOGUE

I SNUCK BACK onto the homestead without anyone noticing. I spent a quiet evening soaking in the hot spring, running only into Sipho on the way back to the lodge. She promised me she was crafting a new lightning charm prototype, but it wasn't up to her standards yet. I told her to take her time, then excused myself. With the world's heaviest eyelids, I went to bed much earlier than I ever do, the sun still streaking into the sky.

Guntram surprised me by waking us both bright and early the next morning. He looked a little tired but more or less acted like his normal self. He offered no apology, nor did he mention our previous fight. It should have irritated me, all these secrets, but given everything I'd been through the last twenty-four hours, I now had secrets of my own.

We were even.

Guntram returned us to our regularly scheduled training. After water warm-up, he decided to try my hand at some fire sigil work. I blew him away by showing him I could stand in fire, no problem.

He accepted my simple explanation that Azar had given me some pointers. I doubt he would have appreciated knowing I'd learned through a trial and error test that almost got me killed. He would have liked it even less knowing I relied on bittersweet memories of Vincent to execute it.

"Well, with water mastery and now fire," he huffed into his beard. "I suppose you have just earth and air left. And lightning too, if we can manage."

I openly groaned. At this rate, I'd be an eyas well past Guntram's age.

But that was the least of my problems. Rafe's bracelet remained on my arm, hidden from view underneath my hoodie sleeve, but I could constantly sense the stirring of strange magic it contained. It hummed in my head long after the headache from the vaettur pith finally receded two days later. I eventually had to take it off and hide it, since Guntram seemed to catch whiffs of the fire charm's energy now and again when we trained. More than anything, I wanted it gone.

But finding an opportunity to slip away without Guntram's notice was easier said than done. His twitchy ravens had their eyes on me constantly. Every time I stepped close to the homestead boundary, a caw would remind me to stay put. I had no way to leave.

Which is why I felt so stupid when I finally remembered I had the power to sneak away whenever I wanted. I waited until after midnight, when

Guntram had fallen fast asleep, before stealing into the lodge kitchen. There, I stood on the counter and extracted the kembar stone from where I'd left it in the highest cupboard.

This time when I appeared in the tiny motel bathtub, I climbed out gracefully. I found Rafe in the upholstered chair, fingers folded in his lap as if he'd been waiting the entire time.

"I heard all about how the mysterious wildfire 'blew itself out.'" A confident smile spread across his face. "I knew you could do it."

I already had the bracelet in my hand. I shoved it toward him. "I came to give you this."

He unlatched the thin metal slat with the fire symbol and pocketed that particular charm. But he declined the rest of his bracelet with a polite raise of his hand. "I'm not ready for them. Not yet."

Startled, I asked, "What do you mean?"

He leaned forward, slapping his hands together in a prayer-like fashion in front of him. "You've only scratched the surface of the things I can teach you about shepherds. Wouldn't you like to learn more?"

I hesitated. Every waking (and most sleeping) moments, I'd been consumed with a nagging worry. How much should I trust the outside world? I already doubted my connection with Vincent. I didn't need that kind of vulnerability in my life. And Rafe? I didn't know what to think of him yet.

Rafe touched my knee softly. "It's okay to hesitate. I waited for a long while too, until I finally had a moment of pure clarity and found my purpose."

Clarity? I snorted. "That must be nice."

"It is. Give me a chance to pass it on to you. Let me teach you. And if you ever feel uncomfortable," he added quickly as I opened my mouth to protest, "you can always leave."

"How can I trust you?" I asked suspiciously.

"Because you have all the power in this relationship, Ina. You are the shepherd. I only have little tricks, a sideshow attraction, compared to what you can do."

"I want to believe you—" I began.

"I do believe in you," he interrupted. "Give me the same courtesy. Believe in me."

I pushed all lingering doubt aside.

"Okay," I said, reattaching Rafe's bracelet to my arm. "Tell me what you know."

WANT MORE INA?

If you enjoyed this *Magic of Nasci* book, read the next in the series:

SHATTERING EARTH

You can also get a free *Magic of Nasci* short story by subscribing to my newsletter at dmfike.com.

Please also consider leaving an honest review on Amazon for this book. It's one of the best ways you can support an author like me!

ABOUT THE AUTHOR

DM Fike worked in the video game industry for over a decade, starting out as a project manager and eventually becoming a story writer for characters, plots, and missions. Born in Idaho's Magic Valley (you can't make this stuff up), DM Fike lived in Japan teaching English before calling Oregon home. She loves family, fantasy, and food (mostly in that order) and is on the constant look out for new co-op board games to play.

More places to keep in touch:

Website: dmfike.com

Email: dm@dmfike.com

Facebook: facebook.com/DMFikeAuthor

Amazon: amazon.com/author/dmfike

BookBub: bookbub.com/profile/dm-fike

GoodReads: goodreads.com/dmfike

MAGIC OF NASCI SERIES

Ina is a rookie nature wizard, learning the ropes of elemental magic—fire, air, earth, and water. She can also wield lightning, setting her apart from the other shepherds of Nasci. This action-packed urban fantasy series takes you on Ina's adventure to prove herself, deep within the heart of the Pacific Northwest forests, where true power still thrives.

BOOK 1: CHASING LIGHTNING

BOOK 2: BREATHING WATER

BOOK 3: RUNNING INTO FIRE

BOOK 4: SHATTERING EARTH

BOOK 5: SOARING IN AIR

APPENDIX: NAMES AND TERMS

This section contains a glossary of Nasci-specific terms and characters with pronunciations, presented in alphabetical order.

Augur (AW-ger): The second highest mastery in the shepherd hierarchy. Augurs have complete control over one element, have a special link to their kidama species, and can train eyas-level shepherds.

Azar (uh-ZAHR): A talented fire shepherd.

Banish (BAN-ish): To send a vaettur back to Letum using magical means.

Baot (bout): A water shepherd who spends most of his time in the Pacific Ocean.

Bitai Wilds (bee-TAHY wahylds): The ecological region of desert encompassing the American West and Mexico that is overseen by a specific sect of shepherds.

Bound (bound): To seal a shepherd's pithways so that they can no longer access their magic.

Breach (breech): The interdimensional portal vaetturs create to travel from Letum to our world.

Charm (chahrm): An object that stores pith or recreates the properties of a sigil.

Cleft (kleft): An opening in the earth where vitae spills.

Cockatrice (KAH-kuh-tris): A dragon and rooster hybrid vaettur with a Medusa gaze.

Darby (DAHR-bee): A rookie shepherd with a talent for earth magic.

Dryant (DRAHY-ant): An animal with magical powers that guards others of its kind or territory. A dryant used to be a normal animal until it was blessed with Nasci's essence.

Etching (ECH-ing): A symbol that is marked on a specific object to give it pith or the properties of a sigil.

Eyas (AHY-uhs): A rookie (and the lowest level) shepherd.

Fechin (FE-chin): Guntram's favorite raven kidama.

Forger (FORJ-er): A follower of Nasci who can sense the four elements (earth, fire, air, and water) and redirect them into objects.

Golem (GOH-luhm): A creature made of pure pith.

Guntram (GOON-trahm): Ina's mentor and master air augur. Ina sometimes calls him Jichan (JEE-chahn), which means "Gramps" in Japanese.

Haggard (HAG-erd): A derogatory term for a shepherd that began training after puberty.

Homestead (HOHM-sted): A secret base with farms and other resources that shepherds visit to rejuvenate themselves and gather supplies.

Ina (EE-nah): A rookie shepherd with mysterious lightning powers. Her real name is Imogene Nakamori (IM-uh-jeen Nah-KAH-moh-ree).

Jortur (JOR-ter): One of Tabitha's favorite black-tailed deer kidama.

Kam (kam): Sipho's female, dark-coated mountain lion who's active at night.

Kappa (KAHP-pah): An aquatic humanoid frog vaettur.

Kembar stones (KEM-bahr stohns): Two stones that are linked like wisp channels.

Ken (ken): Magical sight granted by Nasci that allows a person to sense pith and see vaetturs and dryants.

Khalkotauroi (kal-koh-TOU-roi): A fiery bull vaettur.

Kidama (kee-DAH-mah): A species of animals that augurs can communicate with telepathically and give orders to.

Letum (LE-tuhm): The realm where the vaetturs originate.

Mishipeshu (mi-shee-PE-shoo): An aquatic feline vaettur with mysterious powers.

Nasci (NAHS-kee): The goddess that lives in the center of the Earth who grants elemental powers to her followers.

Nur (ner): Sipho's male, light-coated mountain lion who's active during the day.

Onyara Wilds (ohn-YAHR-ah wahylds): The ecological region of temperate deciduous forests of the Eastern United States that is overseen by a specific sect of shepherds.

Oracle (OR-uh-kuhl): The highest level of shepherd who leads all shepherds within a Wilds territory.

Pith (pith): The essence of fire, earth, air, or water that can be converted into magical energy.

Pithways (PITH-weys): A magical system that

shepherds have inside their bodies to redirect and store pith.

Rafe (reyf): A mysterious stranger who shows up in the woods.

Ronan (ROH-nuhn): An antlered harbor seal dryant that lives on the Oregon coast.

Shepherd (SHEP-erd): A follower of Nasci who can store the four elements (earth, fire, air, and water) in their bodies and cast them using sigils. Also the third highest mastery of shepherd, just above an eyas.

Shepherd Trial (SHEP-erd TRAY-uhl): A rite of passage an eyas takes before becoming a full-fledged shepherd.

Sigil (SIJ-il): A symbol drawn in the air by shepherds to convert their pith into a specific magical spell.

Sipho (SI-foh): The forger of the southern Talol Wilds homestead.

Sova (SOH-vah): A northern spotted owl dryant with metallic mauve streaks in her wings.

Tabitha (TAB-i-thuh): Darby's mentor and master earth augur.

Talol Wilds (tah-LOL wahylds): The ecological region of temperate rainforests stretching from British Columbia to northern California that is overseen by a specific sect of shepherds.

Vaettur (VEY-ter): A predatory creature from Letum that enters our world to devour pith via animals and dryants.

Vincent Garcia (VIN-suhnt gahr-SEE-uh): A game warden for the Oregon State Police.

Vitae (VEE-tahy): The lifeblood of Nasci used to create new dryants.

Wisp channel (wisp CHAN-el): Glowing lights that shepherds use to teleport large distances.

Yoi (YOH-ee): The Oracle of the Talol Wilds.

Zibel (ZAHY-bel): A shepherd who spends most of his time in the Oregon Dunes.

ACKNOWLEDGE-MENTS

Writing a book is one thing, getting it out to the world is another. I'd like to thank those who read early versions of this story, including Jennifer Marshall and Sandra Schiller. You helped shape Ina into the awesome shepherd she has become.

Many talented people gave this book the professional care it deserved. I found my editor Lori Diederich through the 20Booksto50K Facebook group, an invaluable resource for new writers. Sara Smestad modeled for Danan Rolfe so we had plenty of great photos to choose for the cover.

A few final shout-outs. One to my first fan, Samantha Marshall, who believed before anyone else. The last goes to Jacob Fike, who lends both his time and skills to making each of my books better. I couldn't do this without him.

Made in the USA
Middletown, DE
11 August 2023